ME
MYSELF
I

Praise for Pip Karmel and her acclaimed film

ME MYSELF I

"[A] sweet, thoughtful comedy . . . enormously appealing . . . combines high-flying romantic notions with the nitty-gritty."
—Roger Ebert, *Chicago Sun-Times*

"The film's observations are very much on the money. [Its] accessibility rests on the universality of re-examining one's big what-ifs, something almost everyone does at times, and the comic spin Karmel puts on the neatly structured story makes it go down easily."
—Todd McCarthy, *Daily Variety*

"[*ME MYSELF I* is] directed and written with remarkable self-assurance by first-time feature-film maker Pip Karmel. Karmel's intelligent and deliciously witty screenplay . . . [is] simultaneously acerbic and heartwarming, and always keeps you guessing."
—*Toronto Globe and News*

ME MYSELF I

PIP KARMEL

POCKET BOOKS
New York London Toronto Sydney Singapore

The author and publishers would like to thank the following for use of copyrighted material: Lyrics from "You've Got a Friend" by Carole King copyright © 1971 Colgems-EMI Music Inc. All rights reserved. Used by permission. "What I Like About You" by James Marinos/Michael Skill/Walter Palarmachuk copyright © 1979 Romantics Inc. All rights reserved. Used by permission. "Respect" by Otis Redding. Reproduced by permission of Warner/Chappell Music Australia Pty Ltd and Rondor Music Australia Pty Ltd. Unauthorized reproduction is illegal. "Cheek to Cheek" by Irving Berlin copyright © 1935 by Irving Berlin, copyright © renewed, international copyright secured. All rights reserved. Reprinted by permission. Lyrics from "I'm Gonna Wash That Man Right Outa My Hair" by Richard Rodgers and Oscar Hammerstein II copyright © 1949 by Richard Rodgers and Oscar Hammerstein II, copyright renewed Williamson Music, owner of publication and allied rights throughout the world, international copyright secured. Opening quotation from *The Passion* by Jeanette Winterson, first published in 1987, Bloomsbury Publishing Ltd. Line from *A Fly Went By* by Mike McClintock, Random House Children's Books, a division of Random House, Inc.

An *Original* Publication of POCKET BOOKS

 POCKET BOOKS, a division of Simon & Schuster Inc.
1230 Avenue of the Americas, New York, NY 10020

Copyright © Gaumont 2000

Cover artwork property of Sony Pictures Classics

Published simultaneously in Australia by Allen & Unwin

ISBN: 0-7434-0652-4

First Pocket Books trade paperback printing April 2000

10 9 8 7 6 5 4 3 2 1

POCKET and colophon are registered trademarks of Simon & Schuster Inc.

Designed by Lisa Stokes

Printed in the U.S.A.

For Lena and Peter Karmel

I looked at my palms, trying to see the other life, the parallel life. The point at which my selves broke away and one married a fat man and the other stayed here, in this elegant house, to eat dinner night after night from an oval table. . . . Perhaps our lives spread out around us like a fan and we can only know one life, but by mistake sense others.

—Jeanette Winterson, *The Passion*

ME MYSELF I

The Facts of Life

1

Pamela Drury was twelve years old the day her mother caught her trying to burn her underpants in the backyard incinerator.

"Pammy? What on earth are you doing?"

Pamela turned guiltily. "Nothing!"

Her mother leaned into the incinerator and prodded around with the wrought-iron poker, managing at length to spike the singed underpants through the elastic waistband. She pulled the poker out and held the soiled item in the air, which flapped ungainly in the breeze. Pamela burst into tears and ran into the house.

Clearly, Mrs. Drury had left their little talk a little late, and it was with much back-pedaling that she explained to Pamela the facts of life.

"So, really, you should be pleased. It means you're becoming a woman."

The words were said with as much conviction as could be realistically mustered. Pamela sat glumly on the edge of her bed, staring at the wall until her mother had left the room. Tears streamed down her face as she contemplated another forty years of messy underpants. How could God be so cruel? Why had everybody neglected to warn her that being female was an unfortunate exercise in personal hygiene? How could she ever lead a normal existence with a surfboard wedged between her legs, and wearing three pairs of underpants for safety?

Pamela came to dread P.E. lessons, swimming carnivals, and school excursions with a pathological fear, and she swore that in her next life she was going to be a boy. She hated being a girl. She simply was not cut out for that.

And then, in Pamela's thirteenth year, God said, "Let there be libido."

Life was full of surprises. The first time a boy stuck his tongue down her throat, Pamela was surprised. The moment she'd been feverishly anticipating turned out to involve more saliva than a trip to the dentist, and it didn't come anywhere near the nightly fantasies she shared of being with Robert Redford under the privacy of her Flintstones blanket.

Philip O'Rourke was not an entirely unattractive boy, though he was blighted with more than his fair share of blemishes and could have afforded to wash his hair on a more regular basis. He had an extremely long and active tongue and permanently damp underarms, and he really had no way of competing with the Sundance Kid in the smoldering stakes. The relationship lasted three and a half weeks, which, by the teenage calendar, was considered a decent run. After one school dance, five phone calls, a James Bond movie *(The Man with the Golden Gun),* and multiple diary entries, Pamela sent word via her best friend, Terri, that she just wanted to be friends. All went according to plan. She never saw Philip O'Rourke again.

So it was with a great sense of satisfaction, and not a little relief, that Pamela chalked up her first real boyfriend. Now that she had scored on the board, she had the confidence to set her sights a little higher. She called him Sebastian, but she didn't know his real name. He had clear skin, golden-blond, clean hair, and Pamela adored him from afar. That is, he sat at the back of the bus, and she always got on too late to make it much past the driver's seat. The bus arrived at Pamela's school first, and she would push and shove her way down the aisle to disembark through the back door, in order to pass a little closer to her object of desire. Every day they made fleeting eye contact, and Pamela thrilled to the undeniable electrical charges that flew between them. She was sure he had dry underarms. At night, Sebastian's face blended with Robert Redford's, and each diary entry described in detail the morning bus journey and its intricate erotic tapestry.

Pamela carried her obsession close to her breast. Even Terri was oblivious to her secret passion. Pamela was waiting until she and Sebastian graduated to the next level of their relationship before she went public. And for the moment she was savoring the nonverbal courtship. Weeks passed. A whole term went by. The relationship was never consummated. Words were never exchanged. Sebastian never knew Pamela existed. Some years later, she was to find out that Sebastian's real name was Kevin, and he had been two years her junior, a reality which, in those days, bordered on the obscene.

3

She had just turned fifteen when her less-than-eventful love life took a dramatic turn. It was a stinking-hot day during third semester when Terri delivered the message that Tony Rafter liked her. This marked Pamela's auspicious entrée into the Group. The Group from the Girls' School was an exclusive clique of friends who inhabited the social middle ground between the Dags, Try-Hards, and Rejects on the one hand, and the Druggies and Toughs on the other. The Group was made up of attractive, intelligent girls with an uncanny talent for appearing stupid if there was a boy in their vicinity. The corresponding Group from the Boys' School were attractive young men with lower-than-average IQs and a talent for appearing intelligent if there was a girl in their vicinity.

Pamela had been known to linger on the fringes of the Group, but usually she swung dangerously close to the Dags. She was not well versed in the Group's social mores, did a little too well in class, and had yet to perfect the acting-dumb thing. But when Terri announced that Tony Rafter liked her, her hopes rose immediately. Tony not only ran with the Group; he had a high rating. Pamela felt a rush of excitement. She couldn't quite picture him, but she was sure he was good-looking and, at the very least, would make a prestigious entry in her diary.

Terri was an honorable member of the Group even though she fit none of the criteria. She was short and chubby, covered in freckles, and cared not a hoot for impressing boys, having been raised with four brothers. But she lived along the bus route to the Boys' School, and she had great contacts. It fell to her to transmit messages between the two Groups, and she became adept at facilitating budding relationships, as well as their often abrupt demises. The other girls trusted her implicitly with their love lives and rewarded her by including her in the Group as a kind of royal gofer. They tolerated Pamela only because she came with Terri—until Tony Rafter noticed her, of course, and then she became acceptable in her own right.

Pamela and Terri had been best friends since the third day of kindergarten, when Terri found Pamela alone in the sandbox crying. Pamela was dealing with the realization that kindergarten was not just once but every day and that her privileged life at home with her mother was completely and truly over. It was a nasty shock, and one she was convinced she would not survive, with the same sense of doom she was to suffer through every other transition in her life. Terri was the opposite to Pamela. Already extroverted, she couldn't resist a rescue mission like Pamela. She plonked down in the sand opposite the sobbing four-year-old and watched the tears stream down Pamela's face.

"My name is Theresa Gallagher. I have four brothers, and now Mummy has stopped. Do you want to be my sister?"

Pamela shook her head fiercely. "Go away."

But Terri wouldn't take "no" for an answer.

It had been decreed that Pamela and Tony Rafter would get together at Rebecca McDonald's fifteenth birthday party. Pamela begged her mother to make her a new dress especially for the occasion. It was a bright, striped summer shift with shoestring straps that tied at the shoulders. Pamela spent all her pocket money on a pair of bright yellow cork platform shoes and green eyeshadow. She felt like a million dollars.

As soon as she laid eyes on Tony Rafter, she remembered what he looked like. She had actually been thinking of Tony Pellizari, but it didn't matter. This Tony wasn't the crème de la crème. This Tony had a kind of square head, creepily translucent eyes, and was slightly shorter than Pamela, but he was definitely attractive, in a reptilian kind of way. They mumbled a hello to each other. Then Tony put his arm around her. The other girls looked on with approval. When he kissed her, about ten seconds later, Pamela felt a surge of physical euphoria. Tony's technique washed away the memory of Philip O'Rourke into a dribbly blur. She knew she was in the arms of an expert. She could have made out with Tony all night. In fact, she did. Scintillating conversation certainly wasn't on the agenda. He led her into the garden, laid her down on the grass and stuck his tongue in her mouth while expertly untying her shoestring straps. Then he slid a hand under her dress, up her thigh, and proceeded to explore territory that Pamela's own hands had not yet charted. Pamela promptly snapped her legs shut and guided his hand back above her waist.

She was in a state of permanent excitement for days after that. She knew it wasn't love—they'd hardly exchanged words. But they had exchanged an awful lot of saliva, and that must have counted for something. Pamela also knew she was playing with fire. Tony obviously wanted to exchange more than saliva, and she would have to be on her guard. But wasn't it perfectly reasonable that they should stick to making out, which surely was the best bit after all, and completely risk-free? Look at what became of girls who went all the way—like Jacinta Caley, who disappeared from school last semester without a trace. No, Pamela wasn't going to let an imprudent moment of lust ruin her life. She was destined for better things. So she happened to have her period whenever she saw Tony, and that, naturally, meant the underpants zone was out of bounds.

Although not an intellectual giant, Tony did manage to work out that a three-week-long period added up to an awful loss of blood. Finally, while in the throes of slobbery teenage passion one day after school behind the Girls' School oval, Pamela had to concede that she was no longer unclean, but she protested that now was the worst time to have sex, in case she got pregnant. Tony had come fully prepared for that argument—a strip of Lifestyles was discreetly tucked into one of his socks. He pulled out one packet, unwrapped it, and feverishly fumbled it onto his overexcited appendage. It was then that Pamela realized with utter clarity that there was no way she was going to lose her virginity to a desperate specimen like Tony Rafter. She'd got about as much experience from him as she needed, and more than enough for a good diary entry. Besides, this whole affair was interfering with her schoolwork. She stared at Tony's rubber-clad penis, which stood at the ready, and wondered how she was going to let him down gently. She also observed how unappealing the male genitalia really were—this being her first time witnessed up close. She tried to commit it to memory so she could draw it in her diary. Her disenchantment must have been evident, because it wilted under her scrutiny.

The next morning Terri jumped off the school bus bearing the message that Tony just wanted to be friends. Pamela was furious. She had wanted to tell him first.

Pamela never got so much as a nibble from the boys' Group after that. She later discovered that, in the spirit of friendship, Tony Rafter had put the word out that she was frigid, which was at least preferable to having VD, which was what Mark Steadman said about Tina Walsh after she refused to go all the way. Pamela decided that she was not cut out for running with the Groups, and instead she turned her attention to her career. She was going to have a brilliant one after all, and she'd be rich and famous and travel the world, while the Groups would end up in dead-end jobs, married to one another, with three children before the age of twenty-five.

So as Pamela neared her sixteenth year, she threw herself into her roles as editor of the school magazine, chairperson of the school council, and captain of the debating team. She took Robert Redford off her bedroom wall, replaced him with John Travolta, and gave her Flintstones blanket cover to the Smith family. She even got herself a boyfriend—the last speaker for the affirmative in the "Youth Is Wasted on the Young" inter-school debate. Colin was good-looking, intelligent, witty, considerate, respectful, and earnest. Being studious himself, he didn't take up too much of her time; he never once suggested that they go all the way, and he never once implied that she was frigid. The perfect boyfriend.

Terri, on the other hand, had hooked up with a boy at the end of year ten and was content to finish school with average grades. Her boyfriend was the son of friends of Terri's parents. They had met at church one Sunday, and they had been fucking like rabbits ever since. As far as Pamela knew, Terri was the only girl in the Group who was actually having real sex instead of pretending to. Keith adored Terri, freckles and extra pounds included, and they swore they would be together forever. They were a serious young couple and extremely responsible—Terri could recite the pros and cons of ribbed versus sheer versus peppermint-flavored, and she claimed she could apply a condom with her eyes shut. Pamela was very impressed, and quite content to consider herself sexually active by association.

Robert Dickson 2

The night Pamela first laid eyes on Robert Dickson, she decided to go on the pill. Not that she spoke to him that night, nor would she for another three weeks. But she knew he was the one to whom she would willingly give up her virginity, and she was determined to have it ready for him on a platter. Anyway, if it didn't turn out to be him, there was bound to be someone else. Just as her school days were over, she decided, so, too, were her days of frigidity, if not prudence.

At the end of the first week at university, Pamela and Terri ventured into the campus bar on Friday night, reveling in their newfound adult status, even if they did have to keep their eye on the time—their parents weren't quite convinced of their daughters' instant maturation. The orange geometric carpet smelled of beer and cigarettes, and the motley band playing in the corner was appalling, well deserving of its name, The Deadbeats. But Pamela and Terri didn't begrudge them their lack of talent as they happily swilled beer and bopped energetically to a rather dorky and tentative rendition of "Baby, You're Out of Time." Pamela couldn't keep her eyes off the drummer. Obviously the dark, silent type, he wore black jeans and a faded purple T-shirt with a rip in it that hinted at manly chest hair. He had broody eyes, strong features, and a head of thick, wavy hair. A dreamboat, as Pamela was later to describe him in her diary. He played the drums with intensity, totally absorbed in the music, not the least because it took all his concentration to stay in time.

Terri had eyes for the bass player. He was rather more extroverted than the drummer, jumping around like a wild thing and tossing his dirty long hair from shoulder to shoulder in time to the beat in his head, if not the drummer's. Officially, Terri was still going out with Keith. But Keith had gone away to join the army and had told Terri she was free to see other guys if she wanted to. So much for forever. Terri had cried for a week after he left. Then she had decided to get on with her life, which, to Pamela's surprise, she seemed to be having no trouble doing.

The Deadbeats were still bashing out bad covers of classic songs when Pamela and Terri left the bar, drunk, sweaty, and exhausted, and late for their midnight curfew. They stumbled outside into the quadrangle.

"I think the bass player smiled at me!" Terri missed a step and clung onto Pamela before lurching for the balustrade and vomiting into the stairwell. She hadn't eaten anything all day, in an attempt to lose her chubby-schoolgirl image once and for all. As she threw up the entire night's beer consumption, she wondered whether this liquid-diet thing was going to work.

Pamela held Terri tightly, to stop her falling over the edge of the balustrade as she gagged, satisfied that their adult lives were off to a good start.

Friday nights at the university bar became a ritual in Pamela and Terri's schedule—and the highlight of their week. They learned The Deadbeats' entire repertoire and dominated the tiny, and usually empty, wooden dance floor between where the band played and the men's toilets. It became clear to the musicians that they had groupies for the first time in their not-so-dazzling career. On the fourth Friday, during a break, the bass player sidled up to Pamela and Terri at the bar and grinned cockily at them.

"Seen you two lovely ladies at our gigs before, haven't we?"

Pamela and Terri nodded, embarrassed, trying to think of something intelligent to say.

"It's great music—especially the Rolling Stones stuff."

"And the Pink Floyd."

The bass player took his oversized beer mug from the barman and gulped down the brew, leaving a becoming moustache of froth around his mouth. He wiped it on his arm and burped loud and wetly. "You're never around when we finish our last set, though. Turn into pumpkins at midnight, do you?" He roared with laughter at his dazzling wit. "Hey Dicko! Come and say g'day. These lovely ladies reckon we're better than the Rolling Stones!"

Pamela and Terri exchanged looks, immediately perceiving that the name of the band might well reflect the characters of the band members. As the drummer approached, Pamela dreaded her own imminent disillusionment. His name wasn't a good omen. The bass player slapped the drummer on the back

11

and handed him a beer. "Ladies, Dicko. Dicko, ladies. Oh, and I'm Geoff. They call me Big Bad Geoff for short!" He guffawed again. Terri smiled brightly, while Pamela looked away with embarrassment.

"Hi, I'm Terri, and this is Pam."

The drummer nodded. "G'day." He smiled briefly, then proceeded to roll a cigarette. He didn't say another word until they started the next set. Big Bad Geoff, on the other hand, wouldn't shut up.

Pamela and Terri stayed for the first song of the last set, then made a hurried exit. They ran all the way to the bus stop, doubled over with laughter.

"They call me Big Bad Geoff for short!" Terri mimicked.

They sat down in the gutter and trashed Geoff until they were aching with laughter and on the verge of wetting their pants.

"But the drummer seemed all right, don't you think? I thought I could feel some vibes coming from him." Pamela was still harboring hopes.

Terri shrugged. "Dicko? Well, he didn't seem like a complete dickhead. But he's friends with one, so that's not a good sign."

It was a quarter to one before they realized that the 12:05 bus wasn't coming.

Terri grimaced. "My folks are going to kill me. What are we going to do?"

They started walking the impossibly long route home, hoping that a rare Friday-night taxi would go by. Three blocks away from the university grounds, a 1963 Falcon slowed down beside them. The driver rolled down his window. It was Dicko, the dreamboat drummer.

"Hey."

"Hey."

"Need a lift?"

Pamela and Terri looked at each other, having sworn to their parents that they would never hitchhike.

Terri grabbed Pamela's arm and pulled her toward the car. "We know his name, for God's sake." The backseat was crammed full of drumming equipment, so Terri opened the front passenger's door and leaned in a little drunkenly. "Thanks, Dicko. You'd better drop me off first. I'm closest."

13

Terri pushed Pamela in front of her so that she was forced to sit in the middle of the front seat, up against Dicko. Pamela shoved Terri in the ribs and glared at her, suddenly not so sure she wanted to get so close to him that quickly.

Terri talked all the way to her house, then jumped out of the car. "Thanks for the ride, Dicko." She shut the door and leaned in the opened window and whispered to Pamela. "Don't worry. I'll get the plate number."

The ride to Pamela's house was long and painful. She racked her brain to make small talk. "So, how long have you been playing in the band?"

"A fair while."

"Must be an interesting lifestyle."

"It's okay."

"Who's your favorite band? I mean, besides the Deadbeats!"

"Don't really have one."

Pamela gave up and stared out the window the rest of the way home.

"This is my house," she lied. Her house was up at the other end of the street, but there was no way she could actually get out of Dicko's car in front of it, in case her parents were watching. "Well, thanks, Dicko."

He nodded. "Dickson. It's my surname. Hence, Geoff calling me . . . Everyone else calls me Rob. And to tell you the truth, I think the band sucks. We mutilate every great song ever written. I'm only involved because Geoff talked me into it. And he only started the band because he reckoned it would be a good way to pull in the chicks."

Pamela nodded. "And does it work?"

"Sometimes."

Pamela smiled awkwardly and got out of the car. "Thanks anyway, Dic——Rob. And I don't think the band sucks . . . that much."

Pamela waited for him to drive off. But he didn't. And she couldn't walk into a house that wasn't hers, so she hovered behind some shrubbery like an idiot. She waved him off again and backed away. But the car didn't move. What the hell was he doing? She went back to the passenger's window and poked her head in.

"Thanks. Don't wait for me to get inside. I don't want my parents to wake up, and your engine's a bit noisy, so, if you wouldn't mind . . ."

He was looking pensive. "Actually, it doesn't work. The chick thing. I think Geoff scares them off."

Pamela nodded. "Yeah, well, I can see how that could happen."

They smiled. There was an awkward pause until he put the car back into gear. "See you."

"'Bye."

Pamela waited before she headed toward her house. But, he

did a noisy U-turn at the end of the street, drove back toward her, and rolled down his window. "What's your name again?"

"Pam."

He brought the crawling Falcon to a halt. "Look, I'm going to get pizza. I guess you wouldn't be interested?"

Pamela's parents were going to go absolutely ballistic. It was already two o'clock in the morning. There was no way she could go with him.

"Sure."

They went to La Fontana, commonly known as Charlie's pizza joint. Charlie was a wiry Chinese chain-smoker who, oddly enough, made the best pizza in town, according to Rob. Inside it was dark and smoky. The place was furnished with red laminated tables and plastic checked tablecloths with cigarette burns. The walls were covered with dusty travel posters of Roma and the feature wall was a hand-painted attempt at the Fontana di Trevi. An old black-and-white television flickered soundlessly on top of the fridge, while the radio on the counter played golden oldies day and night.

Charlie wiped down their table with a soggy rag that didn't bear scrutiny. "How are you tonight, Rob?"

"Not too bad, thanks, Charlie. Yourself?"

"Oh, you know. Won three hundred on the fourth. Lost four hundred on the fifth. Bloody horses. I could run faster myself." He squinted at Pamela. "And who's your new friend?"

Pamela smiled. "Pamela."

"Welcome to La Fontana, Pamela. May you bring me better luck."

Rob ordered a carafe of house red, which arrived freshly decanted from the flagon, and rolled himself a cigarette while they waited for the pizza. He noticed Pamela watching him. "Do you want one?"

She shook her head. "Thanks. I don't smoke."

After he'd downed his first glass of wine, Rob became more talkative. After the second, he was positively chatty. It became apparent that he was less a musician than a final-year architecture student. He couldn't even read music. But he was smart and funny and seemed genuinely interested in Pamela's ambitions to become a political journalist.

They polished off a large Charlie's Special between them, and a serving of garlic bread. They were thinking about ordering a second carafe of wine when Charlie approached them apologetically. "Sorry, folks, we're closing."

Pamela looked at her watch. It was after three A.M. She was going to be crucified.

They left the pizzeria and sat in the car kissing and talking until the sun came up. During the stints of conversation Rob would roll a cigarette. Under the heady influence of cheap red wine and burgeoning love, Pamela finally succumbed.

"Can I have a puff?"

He handed her the cigarette. She sucked on it casually and exploded into a violent fit of coughing. Her head started spinning and she had to lean out the window and breathe the cold night air to prevent herself from throwing up on the genuine leather seat. Rob smiled.

Pamela poked her tongue out at him. "How can you bear to smoke these things? They're vile."

He dropped her off around the corner from the Drury household at seven A.M. They took another half hour to say good-night before Pamela tore her lips from his, climbed out of the car, slammed the door, and waved him off in a smoky, bleary, up-all-night daze. Walking back to the house, tired eyes aching from the morning sun, she wondered how she was going to face the wrath of her parents. But she knew that even if they killed her, it would have been worth it.

She lost her virginity, at her own insistence, two weeks later in the Falcon. The actual event was something of an anticlimax, but a necessary hurdle to be jumped, and Pamela was soon to discover that with sex, as with smoking, practice did indeed make perfect. So began a wonderful three-year romance with Robert Dickson, and an addiction to tobacco that would endure far longer.

In the beginning, logistics were a nightmare. The couple had the choice between sex in the Falcon, behind the dunes at the beach, or at Rob's share-house at Dempster Street, with Geoff listening through the walls or "accidentally" walking in on them in the bath. So Pamela found herself a part-time job as a dishwasher in a local Indian restaurant, and she and Terri moved into a share-house at 99 Edith Road with Janine Litski, a blond Early Childhood student from Adelaide. Pamela's parents put up a fight, but in the end they contributed a little to the rent, secretly relieved at not having to lie in bed at night wondering when she would be returning home.

Pamela and Terri spent a morning at Shady Syd's shopping for secondhand furniture for the house, and for the princely sum of one hundred dollars they managed to snaffle a great terrazzo-patterned laminated table with six matching chairs, a fake-leather sofa, slightly cracked, a set of bookshelves, two secondhand mattresses, and a 1930s oak wardrobe with mirrored doors.

Pretty soon a routine developed. Pamela spent Wednesday nights at Robert's house, and he spent most of the weekends at hers. Terri and Janine were cool about Robert, but Geoff was totally persona non grata since the night he made drunken passes at both of them, then puked on the fake-leather sofa. Pamela and Robert were known as the blissful couple, and they were the only constant in a household of fleeting relationships. Janine had a string of drop-dead gorgeous boyfriends with few brains, and Terri was happily searching for the one to make her forget Keith.

It was a heady time of late nights spent smoking dope and cigarettes, having sex, drinking flagon claret, playing records, arguing about the state of the world, drinking cardamom tea on Sunday afternoons, and eating Terri's famous double-chocolate-mousse cake. And, of course, they attended lectures, when absolutely essential. Pamela was less than enthused by campus life, and she became hell-bent on winning a journalism internship with the leading newspaper. She did just that in her second year. Rob finished architecture school and landed a job as an assistant in a large firm, where he wore a suit and tie and became known as Robert. His dream was to go out on his own, or in partnership with Geoff—an idea that Pamela tried to quash as tactfully as she could.

They had intended on a romantic and sophisticated celebration of their third anniversary. But on a whim they decided to go to the Royal Easter Show, instead—well, *Robert* decided, and Pamela grudgingly succumbed to his enthusiasm, consoling herself that at least she might be able to get a story out of the event for the paper. Neither had been to the show since they were kids, and Robert was keen to relive childhood memories. Pamela had less fond memories, like throwing up on herself on the Big Zipper and howling with abject terror in the House of Horrors, but she swore that this time she wouldn't make the mistake of eating three Dagwood Dogs and a stick of cotton

candy before going on the rides. She didn't like the rides anyway, and after one horrifying ride on the roller coaster, she was
content to watch from the ground as Robert whizzed through
the air, thrilling to all the rides that he wasn't allowed to go on
as a ten-year-old.

After he'd made himself feel sufficiently ill, they had to buy
hot dogs and chips and waffles and go watch the wood-chopping,
the rodeo events, the show-jumping, and the vintage car show.
Then to the Clydesdales, the sheep-shearing and the stud bulls,
whose pendulous scrotums had to be seen to be believed. Pamela
finally managed to drag Robert to the carnival-like hoopla and
the laughing clowns, complaining that she had never won a
thing and all she had ever wanted as a kid was one of those ugly
stuffed toys that hung elusively from the top of the stalls. They
spent ten dollars on the clowns, only to be rewarded with a
plastic water pistol, two fuzzy dice to hang on the rearview
mirror of the Falcon, and a fake-diamond ring. Robert tried to
convince Pamela that the game was all rigged, that she was
throwing money down the drain and that no one ever won the
big toys, but she wouldn't listen to reason. She did, however,
give up on the clowns, only to progress to the rifle range,
squinting meanly at the tin ducklings as if her life depended
upon their death.

Two rounds and a rubber spider later, Pamela gave up.
"What am I doing? Any boyfriend worth his salt wins a prize for
his girlfriend—especially on their anniversary!"

Robert took up the challenge and applied himself to throwing a dart at a limp cluster of balloons. Twenty-five dollars later,
the toothless, tattooed, greasy-haired proprietor of the stall
took pity on him, scowling as he called, "It's a winner!" He
waved his long stick with a hook on the end and snagged a toy

19

kangaroo from the top row. Pamela took it into her arms with jubilation. It was perfectly white all over, fluffy and soft, with a red ribbon around its neck, and even a little joey peeping out from its pouch.

Pamela hugged Robert excitedly. "You're my hero!"

A moment definitely worthy of documentation. Pamela asked the toothless tattoo if he would take their photo. He consented without grace. Pamela and Robert stood in front of the stall, arm in arm, proudly holding their trophy in the air. Nobody had to say "cheese!"

They stopped on the way home at Charlie's to complete the day's healthy dining with a dose of pizza and cheap wine. Pamela wouldn't leave her hard-won kangaroo in the car, so she brought it inside and propped it up on the table. When Charlie came to wipe down the plastic tablecloth, she grabbed the kangaroo to save it from the ubiquitous damp rag.

Charlie eyed the toy with amusement. "Won a prize at the show, eh? You got better luck than me today."

Robert smiled wryly as he pulled out his tobacco and paper. "And it didn't cost a cent."

Pamela poked her tongue out at him and held Kanga tightly to her, stroking the joey fondly. On closer inspection, it turned out not to be an entire joey, just a head on a piece of elastic. She found this a little alarming and quickly stuffed it back into its pouch.

Robert licked the cigarette paper, spat out a stray bit of tobacco, handed the smoke to Pamela, and rolled another smoke for himself. Charlie brought their carafe of claret with two glasses, then slapped two stained menus onto the table. "Cannelloni's fresh tonight. Gnocchi, too. Beautiful!"

Robert poured the wine, watching Pamela caress the kangaroo. A look of tenderness passed across his face as he raised his glass. "Happy anniversary."

They clinked glasses, leaned across the table, and kissed, holding their cigarettes to the side.

Pamela sat back in her chair and tried to rub some of the day's grime off her face. "Next year I get to choose what we do. Something romantic."

"What do you mean? Are you accusing me of not being romantic?"

Pamela nodded frankly. "Yup."

After they'd finished their pasta and, since it was a special occasion, ordered tartuffo for two, Pamela emptied their day's winnings onto the table.

"And what are we going to do with the rest of our haul: a water gun, two fuzzy dice, a rubber spider, two pairs of three-D glasses, a packet of wash-off tattoos, a doll on a stick, and a plastic diamond ring?"

Picking up the green sparkly ring, Pamela slipped it cheekily onto her wedding finger. "Well, at least it's a perfect fit."

Robert turned up his nose. "But it's bloody ugly."

"Beggars can't be choosers."

Robert stubbed out his cigarette in the plastic ashtray. "Maybe they can." He reached into the pocket of his leather jacket and placed a red-velvet jewel box on the table.

Pamela froze. "Oh, my God, you bastard! You got me an anniversary present. But I didn't get you anything!"

"No, I didn't. It's not really a present. Open it."

Pamela opened the box to find a plain gold wedding band. She stared at it.

Robert shifted nervously in his seat. "I don't know if this is romantic enough for you. But I was wondering . . . I thought . . .

well, we've made it through three years together, and now that I've got the job and everything, I'm pretty secure . . . and I thought . . ."

Pamela looked to him.

"Oh, hell, will you marry me?"

She looked from him back to the ring, speechless.

"Well?"

She swallowed. "Wow."

She knew she should be leaping into his arms and saying yes. She didn't know why she was hesitating. But in a flash she saw two paths stretched out in front of her, and suddenly the right way wasn't clear. She adored him and wanted to marry him and live the whole dream. But she was still young and he was her first, and she had other dreams, too.

Robert looked expectantly at her.

She tried to say something sensible, but faltered. "I'm sorry, I'm bursting to go to the toilet. Won't be long."

She pushed her chair back from the table and made for the ladies' toilets, leaving Robert alone with a glass of claret and an open jewel box, waiting for her answer.

Thirteen and a Half Years Later

3

S uper model!"

"Talk-show host!"

"Genetic engineer!"

An energetic bunch of teenage girls hurl their answers at Pamela, youth oozing from every pore of their hormone-sensitive skin.

"Hang on!" Pamela hurriedly inserts a cassette into her tape recorder, props it up on the front desk, and presses Record.

"Something in the travel industry!"

"Beauty technician . . . one day have my own shop."

"I want to be either a fashion designer or . . . a philosopher!"

"Rich and successful."

"I'm going to marry my hunky boyfriend, Jared, and have four kids."

At this, the other girls groan and whoop censorially, only to be met by a defiant glare.

Pamela smiles. "So what do you think about marriage and kids?"

She looks to a fifteen-year-old with short-chopped hair and braces who hasn't spoken yet.

The girl screws up her face. "Yeah, I want to get married and have a family and all that, but, like, not straightaway."

The others jump in. One says, "But I don't reckon you should let it go too late, like my auntie did. You should see her. She's desperate!"

Another says, "Yeah, you end up old and dried up, and then no one wants you!"

There is general agreement and laughter. Ever the professional, Pamela forces herself to smile with them, so as not to break the rapport. There was a time when she felt a special affinity with teenagers. At this minute she feels a greater affinity with a bag of home-brand dried fruit that has passed its use-by date.

Slamming the car door shut, she grimaces as another piece of rust flakes off the body. At a piercing rendition of the "William Tell Overture," she juggles her belongings, feels the pockets of her leather jacket, and manages to retrieve her miniature cell phone just in time for it to stop ringing. She has not yet worked out how to program it to ring for more than three bars, and she makes a mental note to attempt to read the instruction manual. Flipping the phone open, she reads the message display as she hurries down the busy inner-city street. She punches in a number as she waits to cross the street.

"Allen Sanderson, please . . . Pamela Drury."

The light changes, the crossing signal flashes, and Pamela automatically steps off the curb and crosses.

"Hello, is this Allen? . . . Hello? . . . Hang on, I'm losing you. . . . Can you hear me? . . . Shit!" She flips her phone shut, puts it back in her pocket, and makes another mental note—to change networks—as she runs up the steps of a gray-concrete building, breathing deeply as she passes through the perennial cluster of exiled smokers who huddle under the eaves.

She takes the stairs up to the fifth floor, not only because the elevator is frighteningly unreliable, but also because she vaguely hopes that doing so will alleviate the guilt of an unused gym membership. At the very least, it reminds her she is unfit, so that must be good.

She dumps her bag on her desk, then shrugs off her leather jacket and rifles through her overflowing in-tray, unearthing a packet of nicotine chewing gum. Frantically chewing two pieces of gum at once, she perches on her chair, her heart still racing from the exertion of climbing the stairs.

Pamela's chaotic desk is a microcosm of the scrambled open-plan office that is *Focal Point,* the monthly journal bursting with hard-hitting social and political commentary that she joined too many years ago. Back in the days when black and white were poles apart and "integrity" didn't sound like the name of the latest-model hatchback. Now, as she fights evil and eats cheap lunches, she finds herself wondering why she hasn't done better. Why hasn't she sold out? Somebody has to write for the masses. Somebody has to make the big bucks and drive new European-made cars and live in the eastern suburbs. What's the good of credibility when you're at home alone scraping the moldy wallpaper off your one-and-a-half-bedroom renovator's nightmare?

More and more, as she single-handedly combats environmental disasters and ethnic cleansings, Pamela catches herself glimpsing another scenario. What would her life have been like had she been a little less high-minded (as her mother liked to put it)—if she had had fewer bloody principles? Where would she be now if she'd chosen to change the system from within?

There are a lot of variables in her vision of the other life, depending on the day, but a spectacular harbor view from a forty-fourth floor office invariably is a highlight, not to mention an array of attractive, available men. As opposed to the unattractive available ones . . . or the attractive unavailable ones—not to mention the unattractive unavailable ones that seem to abound at *Focal Point*.

What doesn't feature in Pamela's Utopian vision is Sally, her personal assistant. A twenty-year-old with purple lips and dreadlocks, Sally has rings and studs punched through every punchable part of her anatomy, several of which are not visible in the normal course of daily events and don't bear thinking about. She's bright and cheerful and bursting with enthusiasm, if not competence. Sally makes Pamela feel positively ancient, which is traumatic for someone who is still coming to terms with the passing of adolescence.

Sally stands at Pamela's desk, her arm plastered with Post-it notes. She proceeds to stick the messages in a row on her desk. "That's a no. That's a no. That's a maybe, but I think it will be a no. Green Oaks High said tomorrow's no good, try ringing back next year. The Personal Growth teacher at North Girls' canceled. Presbyterian Girls' School has banned you since that piece you did on their Year Eight drug dealers. Your dry cleaning is ready to be picked up. And your mother called."

Pamela groans as she pulls the cassette from her tape

recorder. A tangled spaghetti of tape spews out. "Shit! Shit! Shit! How am I meant to work with this piece of crap!" She grabs a pen and starts hand-winding the chewed-up tape. A phallic piece of molded Lucite lands on her desk.

"Another bloody award."

Max settles on a corner of her desk. A balding Irishman with a penchant for sticky buns and knitted vests, Max's spongy exterior belies his toughness as chief editor of *Focal Point*.

Pamela barely glances up, feigning indifference. "What for?"

"Your teen-suicide number. Tedious, isn't it? You must have enough bookends to sink a ship by now."

Pamela deposits her chewed gum on the pointy bit of the award statue and smiles wryly. This is the closest Max gets to saying congratulations.

Max squints disapprovingly at her messages. "Jesus, Pam, you're not still researching that story on girls, are you?"

She winces. "I know, I know, deadline's looming."

"*Second* deadline."

Max hovers. Pamela looks up. "Is that all?"

He sucks in his breath. "Actually, no . . ."

"If it's Joe's domestic-violence story, I'm going through it with him tomorrow."

"No, it's not that. It's . . . er . . . something else."

Max shifts a little uneasily. Something tells Pamela she should be on red alert. Her heart sinks. She thought he had agreed not to get personal during business hours. Ever since his drunken declaration of love at the Literature Board lunch, there has been a regrettable tension between them. Why is it that the men you have no interest in whatsoever are always the ones who throw themselves at your feet? It's not that Max doesn't have a certain gruff charm or that Pamela isn't terribly fond of him; it's just that she feels she hasn't been reduced to accepting baldness, sticky-bun guts, and knitted vests just yet. So she had taken him to lunch and told him very honestly and forthrightly and without mincing words . . . that she was involved with someone else. That had done the trick, and since then only when alcohol was on tap did he ever refer to it again.

Pamela checks his eyes and sniffs the air. No sign of alcohol. Possibly not a red alert, after all. Then she becomes aware of the tension in the rest of the office. Sally has slunk off and the others are trying to appear busy, clearly avoiding Pamela's looks.

She turns to Max. "Well?"

He hesitates. "I don't quite know how to put it. . . ."

"Haven't got all day, Max."

He regards her solemnly. "Well, actually, it's not just me. It's the whole office. There's something . . ."

Pamela tenses. "Look, I know I've been a pain in the butt lately, but it's been seventeen and a half days and I'm doing really well and I'm not going to take up smoking again just to make your life easier. Okay?"

Max nods. "It's just that the girls wanted to know how many candles to put on your cake."

Pamela freezes.

"*Happy Birthday!*"

Champagne corks pop and cheers resound. Max raises his glass to Pamela. She shoots him a look that could kill. "You're dead, Max."

Max professes innocence. "Don't look at me! Rog organized the whole thing."

Roger, a pockmarked young journo at the next desk, grins wickedly and holds out his glass for some champagne. Sally sweetly presents Pamela with a gift-wrapped box of aromatherapy oils to treat stress, anxiety, and unresolved anger. Pamela wonders why she didn't throw in misery, despair, and hopelessness for good measure. The "girls" present her with a cruelly calorific chocolate cake, totally covered with what she fears to be exactly the right number of burning candles. She drags a smile onto her face, takes a deep breath, and attempts to extinguish them as rapidly as possible.

The revelry is interrupted when a stranger enters the office. Tall, black, and more than handsome, he sports a well-cut suit, button-down shirt, and silk tie. Certainly not the normal, pallid *Focal Point* fare. The room settles into a hush of wonderment.

"Pamela Drury?"

A resonant, deep, authoritative voice. Everyone looks to Pamela. She waves weakly. "Yes?"

The vision of manliness approaches her desk.

She draws a blank. "Sorry, did we have an appointment?"

The man nods. Frowning, Pamela flips open her planner. As she scans the day's entries, loud music kicks in. In one deft movement the stranger tears off his suit jacket, complete with shirtfront and tie, revealing a glistening, muscle-rippling torso. Pamela screams and covers her face in agony. Everyone else shrieks with laughter. She turns to Roger and snarls at his smug countenance. Gyrating lustily to the music, the stripper divests himself of his trousers, proudly showing off a body designed by God and built by the City Gym. The girls squeal and clap.

The music heats up and the stripper proceeds to climb onto Pamela's desk. She swiftly pulls her laptop to safety. The office staff whoops and whistles as the stripper thrusts his leopard-skin, vacuum-packed butt into Pamela's face. Try as she might, she can't help inhaling the pungent mixture of sweat and Polo

Sport by Ralph Lauren. He turns and grins seductively as he slowly peels his leopard spots off to wild applause. Pamela pelts them at Max, who, overcome with jungle fever, promptly adorns his balding head with them. Pamela leans back in her chair, desperate to evaporate into the ether.

All that remains between her and the glistening Adonis is a bulging red-sequined G-string, and, to her horror, he seems determined that it should end up between her teeth. She closes her eyes. How did she come to this?

"Go on, you take it, Pamela."

"No, really, it won't get eaten. You take it."

She pushes away the remains of the chocolate cake, complete with pile of melted candles. If there's one thing more depressing than a birthday cake, it's leftover birthday cake sitting in your fridge for a week.

She tries to make an unobtrusive exit, but to no avail. Max lurches toward her, champagne in hand. "So, what do you say? You gonna let me show you the night of your life?"

She smiles brightly. "Sorry, Max. Prior engagement!"

Max nods and takes another gulp of champagne. Pamela consoles herself with the fact that, for once, she is telling him the truth.

It is dusk when she emerges from the Kleen Machine Laundromat, a week's supply of washing and dry cleaning in her arms. It really is an extravagance, but she just can't bring herself to face the communal laundry in her block of flats. Not since she found a used syringe in the dryer. She's had visions of pulling on her jeans one morning and suffering a needle prick. Of course, it's a totally ridiculous flight of paranoia, but then again it would be just her luck to be the only person in the world to contract AIDS from a clothes dryer.

Next door to the laundromat is La Fontana, the same run-down pizza joint that Pamela and Rob used to frequent all those years ago. Neither the pizzeria nor Charlie has changed at all, except for a general increase in tobacco stains. Since moving back into the neighborhood, Pamela has become a regular customer of Charlie's take-away menu. Charlie was delighted to meet up with Pamela after so many years and takes a paternal interest in her well-being. He never could understand why she didn't marry Robert Dickson, and he reminds her constantly that she shouldn't be sitting at home, single, eating take-away pizza.

Today he sits at one of the faded red laminated tables on the sidewalk. Cigarette hanging from his lips, he is absorbed in his Lotto cards. Pamela attempts to open her car door without dropping her dry cleaning in the gutter.

Charlie looks up. "Hey, Pamela!"

"Hey, Charlie."

"Give me a number."

Pamela scowls. "Thirty-five."

He scrutinizes his cards. "I got it already."

"Going on forty." She bundles her wash into the car. For as long as she can remember, Charlie has been trying to luck his way out of pizzas. No doubt about it—he's a throwback to his forebears who came from China looking for fortune in the gold-rush days. Only now, prospecting for gold has given way to Go Lotto, Scratch Lotto, and the TAB. And in the meantime, the Chans, sixth-generation Australians, supported their prospecting by opening an Italian trattoria. That was back in the days when pizza was the newest rage since honey prawns.

31

"Have you ever won a single cent on those things, Charlie?"

Detecting a trace of cynicism, he looks at Pamela with reproof. "You know you're looking at a very nearly rich man. You know that? Few years back, all my numbers came up."

This is news to Pamela. "All of them? I don't believe you."

"All I had to do was add one. Twenty-six dropped in. I had twenty-seven. Eighteen, I had nineteen. Every single one! Five, I had six. Two—"

"You had three."

Charlie stubs out his cigarette mournfully. "I tell you, it was something. If only the world had shifted its arse by one. You know where I'd be now? Somewhere else. Driving a Ferrari. You coming in for some gnocchi? Fresh this morning."

Pamela starts the car. "Not tonight, Josephine!"

"Don't you go getting too skinny. You don't look after yourself! You never have. You should be married."

She has heard it all before. "*Ciao*, Charlie."

He waves her away with mock ill temper.

Despite its being her birthday, she has a good feeling. For a start, it's not every day that she gets a parking spot right in the front of her block of flats. In fact, she can't remember it ever happening before. It's got to be an omen. Maybe that "You Can Change Your Life—A Practical Guide to Positive Thinking" workshop is really starting to bear fruit. Yes, she has an intuition that something good is just around the corner. Maybe tonight's the night that her whole life has been traveling toward. Maybe the glass is half full, after all.

Loaded up with her briefcase and laptop, groceries, the laundry, the dry cleaning, a bunch of birthday balloons, and a red sequined G-string, she wrenches a wad of junk mail from the dilapidated letter box at the entrance of a distinctive 1940s redbrick apartment block. Maneuvering her awkward load through the glass doors, she steps on her dry cleaning, trips over her shopping, drops the mail, and lets go of the balloons, which float up through the stairwell and come to rest at the ceiling. Pamela watches the balloons, then drops everything and sinks to the floor. She is struck by a vivid mental picture of a glass, half empty, and draining fast.

Loaded up again, she trudges up the stairs to the top floor, not to get exercise, and not because the lift is out of order, but because there isn't one. She tries not to breathe in too deeply as she detects in the air a fresh melange of cats' piss and dampness. Or has the reclusive old lady in number four finally kicked it? After all, that would be the only giveaway. The smell. Pamela has a flash of herself forty years on, lying on the bathroom floor, hip broken, flannel nightie askew, hot-water bottle leaking beside her. She shudders, then hurries past number four.

Reaching the top floor, she nods to the escapee balloons bobbing above her. One of them has already had an unfortunate run-in with the ceiling light and hangs torn and limp from the ceiling.

"Serves you right."

She anchors the balloons with her briefcase. The phone is ringing as she struggles with the key in the lock. As she elbows her way through the door she can hear herself rattling off a convoluted greeting.

"Hi. You've reached my machine, but I'm afraid the rest of me isn't with it, so please send a fax or leave a message in a clear voice after the beep and I'll get back to you as soon as I can. Alternatively, you can try me at work on 9875 8811, e-mail me on

pam@net.com.au, or catch me on my mobile on 0411-346-3."—
Beep.

She drops her load and races to the answering machine.

"Pam, just your old mum, ringing to wish you the best, but you're not there, so let's hope you're out celebrating. Well, happy birthday, love."

The machine clicks off. She bites her lip and presses Delete.

"I uv und ahoove o' mythelf . . . I uv und ahoove o' mythelf."

Pamela's words are indistinct as she intently flosses her teeth in front of the rusted bathroom cabinet. The cabinet is plastered with a series of cut-up index cards featuring hand-written affirmations highlighted in fluorescent marker pen. She winds the used dental floss around a square of toilet paper and drops it in the bin.

"I love and approve of myself."

Leaning into the mirror, she studies a looming pimple and debates whether to squeeze.

"I am in the rhythm and flow of ever-changing life."

She wraps a towel around her wet hair and pulls on her trusty old terry-cloth bathrobe. On the basin is propped a pho-tograph of Allen Sanderson, dark and handsome, smiling allur-ingly. Pamela picks him up and gazes into his seductive eyes.

"I deserve the best and I accept the best. I deserve the best and I accept the best."

In the bedroom, rifling through her underwear drawer, she seizes the black-lace bra that gives cleavage, but not too much, and searches for a matching pair of underpants with elastic still intact. She rips open a new packet of sheer stockings, pulls them on, confronts herself in the mirror from every angle, pulls them off, and opts for her old opaque pantyhose.

"Coward."

Dressed in her matching lace underwear, and hobbling on one high-heeled shoe, she frantically searches the living room but is impeded by its state of utter disarray, the result of long-incomplete home renovations. The messy process of painting and stripping has meant that the entire contents of the room has been pushed into the center, creating a congested living area that has been steadily gathering dust for the last ten months. Despite all evidence to the contrary, she'd managed to delude herself that she was possessed of a dormant renovating gene that would be activated by the acquisition of real estate, a delusion that lasted as long as it took to buy all the materials, start the work, and make an uninhabitable mess.

She checks under piles of packing boxes and drop cloths, behind stacks of framed pictures and furniture, while the television fires questions at her.

"Which nineteenth-century poet wrote 'Ode to a Nightingale'?"

"Keats."

She searches among the relics of adventures past—artifacts and mementos from exotic climes: African sculpture, South American tapestries, Pacific island masks, a stuffed llama, a large cardboard model of the Empire State Building . . .

"When was the USSR dissolved?"

"December 19 . . . 91!"

Groping under the couch with one arm, a complex network of cobwebs is disturbed, sending a family of daddy-long-legs scampering.

"Famous for its giant stone statues, Easter Island, in Polynesia, is known by its original inhabitants as—"

"Rapa Nui!"

Triumphant, she emerges with the renegade shoe.

In her favorite little black dress and ivory-silk embroidered coat, she parades in front of the mirrored wardrobe door that leans against the same 1930s oak wardrobe she bought at Shady Syd's to furnish the bedroom of the house in Edith Road that she'd moved into with Terri in their first year at university. She had promptly painted it Dulux Sunflower Gloss, to hail freedom and adventure. After she parted ways with Robert Dickson, she'd overpainted the bright yellow with Rich Burgundy, to mark a new chapter in her life. Semigloss Turquoise was the weekend everything was going to change and she was going to connect with her spiritual self. Followed by Matte Black—less a reflection of her state of mind than an unfortunate attempt to conform to the fashion of the time. The last layer, Golden Ocher, had been on special at the local hardware store. Then, one day, just after she'd taken possession of the flat, she took one look at the wardrobe and decided that it was time to grow up. In a flash of enthusiasm she began to restore it to its original state, working feverishly for hours. Twelve months later the can of paint stripper still stands by, together with a glued-up paintbrush and a pile of acrylic-encrusted rags.

She scrutinizes her image in the mirror. *What is it that you have to say these days? Attractive, sexy, confident, open, funny, intelligent—but not scary.* She strains for a back view, then walks up to the mirror and mimes a hello and a bright red lipsticked smile while the television game show prattles on behind her: "Lovely prize, Steve. We're not going to waste any time. If you want to buy: ten dollars. Simple as that. Ten dollars—going once, going twice, going three times. No sale."

Pamela's smile fades.

She checks the contents of her handbag. Tissues, comb, lipstick, mini-toothbrush, a Qantas dental-floss stick . . . She rummages farther and retrieves a condom. Blowing the lint off the wrapper, she squints dubiously at the use-by date.

"Which play by William Shakespeare opens with the words 'Now is the wint—'"

She switches off the television.

"*Richard the Third.*"

After hurriedly turning the answering machine on, she double-locks the door and pulls it shut behind her. Immediately, she unlocks it and goes back in. She checks the turned-off iron. Though she hasn't used it, she disconnects it from the outlet anyway. Taking a deep breath, she exits again, slamming the front door behind her, causing the bathroom shelf to tremble, and Allen Sanderson to fall facedown into the basin.

Seated at a table in a romantic leafy courtyard, she shifts the candle around to give her face the optimum ambience. Satisfied, she traces parallel lines in the fresh white-linen tablecloth with her fork, then starts tapping it in time to the piped Vivaldi wafting from behind the silk wisteria. With a start she realizes she is being watched. Standing opposite her is Allen Sanderson, smiling alluringly. Just like in his photo, except that he appears to be several years older than the photo suggests, several pounds heavier, and has somewhat less hair.

"Pamela."

"Allen."

He smiles again and takes his seat. "How are you?"

"Very well, thank you. And yourself?"

"Can't complain."

They struggle with introductory small talk until they are mercifully rescued by a speedy waiter who thrusts oversized menus at them and launches into a graphic account of the evening's specials. Pamela listens to none of them, instead scanning the menu for something easy to eat that won't splash or get stuck between her teeth. As for garlic, she concedes that she probably won't be able to avoid it altogether, but she concludes that as long as Allen eats some, too, they should cancel each other out. She doesn't know whether to be relieved or alarmed when he orders garlic prawns, a salad of Spanish onion, and a side order of garlic bread. Pamela ends up making a panicked choice of char-grilled octopus and immediately regrets it. The waiter swipes the menus away and disappears, leaving them to themselves. Allen smiles at her. He's used the same smile three times now, and Pamela wonders if that is the extent of his facial repertoire. She watches as he toys with the stem of his champagne glass.

Suddenly, he blurts out at her, "You know, I've never done this before."

Pamela nods uncomfortably. "Oh?"

"I . . . I guess I could go to nightclubs, discos . . . but, I mean, if I was a decent type of lady sitting there minding my own business and a man like me came up and tried to strike up a conversation with me, *I'd* think I was a sleaze. So, I think it's perfectly reasonable that people make use of personal advertisements. Don't you? I mean, I certainly don't think we should feel we have anything to be ashamed of. Do you? We're not freaks. We're not social retards. We're just intelligent, mature people taking our destinies into our own hands. Right?"

He smiles, his forehead glistening with perspiration. He reaches for a cigarette. "Do you mind?"

"Oh, no. No, go right ahead."

He offers the packet to Pamela. She shakes her head.

"No, thanks. I don't . . ."

She watches him light up, desperate to be doing the same. Instead, she demurely sips her wine. "So, Allen, what was it you said you did?"

Later that evening, the sounds of passionate sex emanate from Pamela's apartment. Allen lights up and begins to smoke. Then he begins to crackle. Pamela gives him a final blast of heat from her Heat-n-Strip gun and drops his burning face into the fireplace, where it joins an assortment of smoldering photographs of prospective males and accompanying letters. She reads another one before consigning it to the bonfire: "Dear M112987, From your ad you sound like an interesting, genuine lady."

Still in her evening clothes, she stands at the mantelpiece, Heat-n-Strip gun in hand, while behind her the television emits a torrid sex scene from a Spanish movie, hot-blooded lovers crying out with hot-blooded passion. She pulls the plug out of the wall. "Oh, shut up."

Firing the gun at the windowsill, she attacks the melting paint with a scraper, trying to block out the excruciating image of herself and Allen standing on the street corner outside the restaurant, his face all blotchy, partly because of his allergy to hidden dairy products, and partly because he had burst into tears over the dessert. Pamela didn't have much sympathy for him. If you're going to start dating two weeks after your wife has walked out with the three children . . . She had assumed that her future with Allen was pretty well an oxymoronic concept, so it was a complete surprise when he lurched toward her and kissed her good-night.

"I had a really good time tonight, Pamela. I think you're a very special lady."

She had nodded dumbly. He hadn't asked her a question all night. Maybe he had her confused with the woman at the next table, who had been describing her hysterectomy in less than dulcet tones.

"Oh, yes. Me, too. Thanks, Allen."

"Can I ring you?"

Ah! A classic exercise Pamela had covered in her assertiveness training. Start with something positive. "I really enjoyed meeting you, Allen." Be clear. "But I don't think we're right for each other." Then get out of there. "Thanks for a lovely evening. Good night." Unfortunately, she was a bit rusty.

"Okay."

She backed away. Allen cheerfully waved good-night. Pamela found her car, got in, slammed the door, and banged her head on the steering wheel.

Now she is burning the memory away with the heat gun. Smoking, toxic muck builds up on the scraper. She attempts to shake the goo off, but the goo won't shake, and she's reminded of why her do-it-yourself renovations have not done it themselves. Hot and frustrated, she goes to open the window for some air, but decades of botched-up paint jobs have sealed it shut. She struggles and strains, then gives up.

Slumped on the floor with half a bottle of vodka, she tries to put it all out of her mind. The little black dress and high heels have been usurped by the faithful toweling bathrobe and airline socks, but the lace underwear remains a cruel reminder of the disastrous evening. She takes a swig of vodka, wincing. It

wasn't so bad, really. Not really. Actually, she feels pretty proud
of herself. None of her single girlfriends would stoop so—
would be brave enough to try the Personals. And as they say,
you win some, you lose some. Got to be in it to win it. Nothing
ventured, nothing gained. All work and no play . . . She takes
another gulp of vodka, looking around and wondering whether
the state of her apartment qualifies as a symptom of clinical depression. She guiltily eyes a mountain of cardboard boxes piled
close to the ceiling. They eye her back with disdain. Where are
the long-promised bookshelves?

Tired of waiting for the walls to be painted, one of the
boxes has split open, and a stack of books has escaped through
the side. She squints at the scattered titles through the vodka
bottle: *Heal Your Own Life; 237 Intimate Questions to Ask Men;
Smart Women—Foolish Choices; Women Who Love Too Much; If
I'm So Wonderful, Why Am I Still Single?*.

She closes her eyes and downs the rest of the vodka, sniffing and wiping her mouth on her arm. If it wasn't for the fact
that she is so goddamned miserable, she's sure she'd see the
funny side.

Dragging a dusty cardboard box over to the couch, she
grabs a Stanley knife and drunkenly hacks through the packing
tape to pull out an old chocolate box tied with faded red-satin
ribbon. Hesitating, she unties the ribbon and sorts through
photographs of her boyfriends through the years, discarding
them into the still smoldering ashes as she goes.

"Bastard. Coward. Misogynist. Commitophobe. Dental sur-
geon."

Digging deeper into the box, she finds an ancient cigarette
packet whose contents she shakes out: a Bic lighter and half a
dozen very old, squashed cigarettes that she regards fondly, like

a long-lost lover. She carefully straightens one out, puts it to her lips, and continues on her way, uncovering a vintage Walkman, which she turns over in her hands. God, she remembers buying this—duty-free, on her first trip overseas. No, she lies. She can't exactly remember buying it, but she knows for a fact that a much younger Pamela did buy it on the eve of departure. She hardly recognizes that Pamela anymore, but as she holds the Walkman, she catches glimpses of a younger self riding on a bus through Italy; in a bunk bed in a youth hostel in Munich; on a night train through Egypt, where she met that French boy with the eyes and the lips . . .

She sighs and flips open the Walkman, pulling out an old cassette tape and turning it over curiously. No label. She slots it back in, puts the headphones on, and presses Play. Her head fills with an upbeat song from her past: "Ça Plane Pour Moi," by Plastic Bertrand. More memories flood in. Much jumping up and down, she recalls. She smiles nostalgically and bops to the song.

Lighting the stale cigarette with relish, she pulls from the box more dusty memorabilia: souvenirs from her travels, photo albums, and a brand-new white toy kangaroo. She strokes its fur and peeks into its pouch.

"Hey, Kanga, I thought I gave you to the Smith family."

She leans over and reaches for a tattered diary, and as she opens it, some loose photos slip out into her lap. She picks up one of them and stares at the photo of a handsome young man.

The Walkman batteries give up the ghost, and the song slows to a strangled crawl. Pulling the headphones off, she scrutinizes the photo. Mr. Right. She tortures herself with images of her and Robert Dickson at the height of their relationship. There it is. Hard evidence that they had been deliriously happy. Smiles, laughter, good times. "Robert Dickson," she whispers. "Why did I let you go?"

She stares at a faded photo of herself and Rob posing together in Sideshow Alley, arm in arm, proudly holding up the toy kangaroo she now holds in her arms.

From the back of the diary she tentatively pulls out an aged newspaper clipping and, against her better judgment, unfolds it. It is a segment from the social pages of a regional paper and features a photo of Robert Dickson and his glowing blond bride, Janine Litski, on the steps of St. John's Church. The same Janine Litski, gorgeous blond Early Childhood student, with whom Terri and Pamela shared 99 Edith Road. Robert's ghastly best mate, Geoffrey Ballodero, stands as best man, and some friend of Janine's is the best woman. Pamela squints drunkenly at the bride and mimics her saccharine smile. Janine Litski . . . No—Janine Dickson. She hugs Kanga to her breast and succumbs to a fit of uncontrollable weeping.

Step. Elbow. Punch. 4

Perfect blue skies, glittering harbor water, and the gentle banging of ropes against masts fail to restore Pamela's soggy spirits. She nurses her hangover behind dark glasses, struggling to keep up with Terri, who is power-walking ahead, dressed in the latest lycra gear and power-pushing the latest-model sports pram, complete with large racing wheels and newborn baby. Early-morning joggers, cyclists, and rollerbladers whiz by. Pamela manages to drag herself level with Terri. "I was going to be so successful."

Terri groans inwardly, recognizing today's tone of voice as a number eight on the Drury scale of misery. "What do you mean? You are!"

Pamela shakes her head morosely. "No. I've completely fucked up. You know, you were so lucky to meet Leonard when you did. You got yourself a masculine yet sensitive husband, a fantastic marriage, and to top it off you've got Otto. You're disgustingly happy."

Terri puts her hands up in defense. "So shoot me! Anyway, what's *happy?* You know where it comes from? In here. Attitude."

Terri thumps her chest.

Pamela scowls. "That's easy to say when you're happy."

Terri stops the pram and turns impatiently to Pamela. "Jesus, Pam, you need to reframe."

"Reframe what? What've I got to show for the last ten— God—the last *fifteen* years? Really."

Terri hesitates, and Pamela walks on, satisfied she has proven her point.

Terri watches as her wretched friend moves on. Otto begins to cry and she picks him up and rocks him quiet. It is true that she is happy, but then her disposition has always been more prone to happiness than Pamela's, dating all the way back to kindergarten. The thing is, Terri wasn't born with Pamela's advantages, and Pamela should know it. Pamela had been the bright, attractive one with loads of ambition and a brilliant future, while Terri was the reliable all-rounder with a perpetual weight problem and a natural spring of positive thinking. Unlike Pamela, she hadn't excelled in anything very much since school except the art of meeting life's highs and lows with equanimity. And being a friend to Pamela.

Terri did feel lucky to have met Leonard, but then Pamela just has diabolical instincts when it comes to men. For a highly intelligent and successful woman, she has a disastrous track record with the opposite sex. In recent years Terri has watched her zoom straight to the ones with "bastard" stamped in bold print across their foreheads, has suffered through the high of the heady infatuation and the dreamy plans for the future, and has been there at the end to help scrape up the pieces. Pamela usually bounced back after a month or six and would celebrate her newfound strength and independence with a life-threatening adventure holiday, before hurtling head-first into the next Mr. Wrong. But lately there has been a drought of men, bastards or otherwise, and Terri knows that Pamela is losing heart. Her love life doesn't seem to be so much a game anymore as a race.

Terri hurries to catch up with Pamela. "A challenging, award-winning job on a quality journal . . ."

Pamela sniffs. ". . . that no-one reads."

"A flat of your own, which will be terrific when you pull your finger out and do something with it."

"What for? It'll still be empty."

Her friend battles on. "Freedom to travel all over the world when you want. Independence."

Pamela looks Terri in the eye and grunts bitterly, "Freedom!"

Terri pulls out strange and assorted baby equipment from the pram, while Pamela sits on the sea wall clutching baby Otto awkwardly on her knee and gazing out over the water.

"I think I've missed the boat."

"Where to?"

Pamela doesn't appreciate Terri's obtuseness.

"I'm thinking about having a baby."

Terri looks at her, astonished, and Pamela returns her look defiantly.

"By myself, if I have to."

"I thought you didn't like kids."

"What's that got to do with it?"

Pamela's nose twitches. She lifts Otto up, tentatively draws her face toward his bottom, recoils and hurriedly hands the baby back to its mother with scarcely concealed relief. "Anyway, it's different when they're your own."

Terri regards her skeptically.

"I like Otto."

Terri proceeds to open up Otto's soiled diaper, while Pamela feigns a sudden interest in something in the opposite direction. "You know, I'm supposed to be happily married with two children by now," she declares.

Terri scoffs. "Who says?"

"A clairvoyant."

Terri looks at Pamela in disbelief. "When did *you* go to a clairvoyant?"

"Ages ago. After I decided not to marry Robert Dickson."

Terri raises her eyes heavenward.

"Oh, please! You don't seriously still think about *Robert,* do you? I mean, how many years ago are we talking about? Ten? Twelve?"

"Thirteen and a half."

Terri shakes her head.

"Whatever happened to Dicko?"

"He ended up marrying Janine Litski."

"Oh, my God, that's right! Miss Blond Early Childhood."

Pamela didn't need to be reminded. "Anyway, this clairvoyant said to move on, don't look back, and I'd meet a wonderful man and have two great children by the time I was . . ." She looks away, lip trembling. "Well, by now."

The business day starts off on a brighter note. No sooner has Pamela switched on her laptop and popped a Nicorette into her mouth than Sally bounces up to her desk. "I've got you into a school. You have to be there in half an hour."

Pamela closes her computer. "Great. Thanks. Where is it?"

"Rooty Hill. I left a message on your machine. I guess you didn't get it. It sounds quite interesting. A girls' kung fu class or something."

"Rooty Hill? I can't get there in half an hour! Where's the address?"

Sally apologetically hands her a Post-it-note. Pamela grabs it and runs as Sally calls after her, "I tried to call your mobile, but the voice-mail thingy still isn't on."

Pamela groans, sickened by the thought of all the life-changing calls she's probably missed through her own incompetence. There's no avoiding it. She's got to read the manual.

She can't remember driving this far west in her life. Sally seems to specialize in locating the most remote high schools in Sydney. Even when she has plenty of time, Pamela always manages to get lost. City dweller that she is, suburbia is alien territory. She struggles with the street directory while trying to stay on the freeway, knowing that to take the wrong exit would be to spin off into orbit around a galaxy of housing estates.

Miraculously, she's only forty-five minutes late when she slips into the back of a 1970s cream-brick school hall. Despite the heavy security grilles on the windows, years of vandalism have left few of the furnishings intact. She chooses a plastic, grafitti-covered seat without chewing gum on it and settles down to watch what's left of the action. A motley group of adolescent girls practices the application of an elbow jab to the stomach, followed by a fist to the groin of an invisible assailant. They work in pairs with faded red body protectors, while their teacher, an energetic man in his early thirties, bellows at them. "Come on! There's no point being ladylike. Show him you mean it. . . . no! no!"

The girls rejoin feebly, "No . . . no."

Groaning, he demands a stronger response. Pamela watches from the side, notebook at the ready, and idly notices that the slightly sweaty and disheveled teacher is unmistakably attractive. She scans her pad for the contact name Sally gave her. Ben Monroe. Good name. Strong. Sexy. Probably gay, and definitely not available.

Ben moves around the class.

"Okay. Let's say he's got hold of you. What are some of the things you've learned that you could use?"

"Kicking?

"Punching."

"Elbowing . . . Yell!"

"Head-butt him?"

Ben nods. "And what if he's got you on the ground? On top of you?"

A girl with terrible acne raises her hand. "Pretend to cooperate, then bite off his tongue."

Her friends nod approvingly.

"Stick your finger in his eye."

Ben is not satisfied. "Anything else?"

The class shrugs. Ben searches their faces. An apathetic silence. Pamela calls out. "Rupture his scrotum?"

The girls turn and look at her, as does Ben. The piercing sound of an electronic buzzer breaks the moment and the class turns into a rowdy rabble as they throw down their protectors, grab their bags, and get the hell out of there.

Pamela approaches Ben as he piles up the gym mats. "Does that stuff really work? All that yelling?"

"Sure. A bit of elbow power can go a long way. Here, try me."

He turns toward her and she steps back. "No, it's all right. I carry a gun."

He smiles. "At all times? Step to the side. Elbow. Punch. It's easy." He grabs her matter-of-factly and she stiffens. "Say someone's got you from behind. Step. Elbow. Punch."

In the cause of research, she tells herself, Pamela goes through the routine, albeit apprehensively, keenly aware of the warmth of his body and his not altogether unpleasant aroma.

Ben corrects her footwork. "Again."

She repeats the move, not at all convinced of its efficacy.

"Okay. Now use you lungs. Give it all you've got."

She gives it all she's got. *"No!"*

Elbow. Punch. Ben is knocked backward onto the floor under the force of the blow.

Amazed, Pamela eyes him suspiciously. "Did you do that?"

He shakes his head emphatically as he nurses his groin, and she grins. "Wow. Sorry."

Standing in the doorway of a congested storeroom she watchs Ben pack away the body protectors and tries to remember what she's there for. "So, do you think girls get a fair go at this school?"

"Nope. No one does." He looks at her, bemused. "What's this for again? I wasn't told."

Pamela realizes Sally has been slack with the setup, and she makes a mental note to rip out her navel ring. "*Focal Point.* An article about girls in today's world. Their dreams, ambitions. What they see as their major obstacles."

Ben nods. "Good stuff. *Focal Point.* Great articles."

"You read it?"

"I can, you know."

51

She stammers. "No, I didn't mean . . . it's just . . . I didn't think it's the kind of reading . . . that a P.E. teacher . . ."

Ben looks quizzically at her.

"P.E. teacher? Oh, no, this isn't phys.ed. This is Life Skills."

"Oh, so you're . . . ?"

"Student Crisis Counselor, resident punching bag. Ben. Ben Monroe." He extends his hand.

Pamela hesitates, then shakes his hand in a businesslike fashion. "Pamela Drury."

He unzips his bag and grabs a pullover. "There was a terrific article a while back, on teen suicide."

"Thanks."

He stops, pullover half pulled over. "*You* wrote that?"

"I can, you know."

Touché.

Ben is clearly impressed. "I wish I'd made a copy of it. Somebody swiped it from my office. Probably some poor suicidal kid who thought it was a how-to guide. Do you reckon I could get hold of a back copy?"

Her thoughts collide. *Is he serious? Why would he want a back copy? He's just trying to flatter me. But why would he want to do that? No, it's a genuine request. He's a counselor, for God's sake. It's probably nothing. . . .* She's an idiot to think. Still, is there something in the air, or is it her imagination?

"A back copy? Of the teen-suicide story? Yes, I think so, if you really want . . ."

He closes the door and locks it. "Nearly went that way myself, you know."

Pamela's brow furrows with concern. "Suicide?"

Ben smiles. "Journalism. Investigative, of course. Ask the hard questions. Expose corruption. Right all wrongs."

Pamela smiles weakly, trying to remember the last wrong she'd righted.

Ben opens the reinforced-glass door. Heavy-duty graffiti adorns the walkway, and there are few windows unbroken. He gestures for Pamela to go first. They pause, a little awkwardly. She wills him to say something.

"Uh . . . look . . . if you ever need to do any more research . . ."

Yes! Pamela nods, as professionally as she can. "Thanks. That'd be great. It can be a real hassle getting into schools."

"I'm a bit hard to catch here." Ben reaches into his pocket and finds some paper. "You don't have a . . . ?"

She scrambles in her bag for a pen and hands it to him, stepping aside to let some murderous-looking students pass. Ben jots down his details. "We get the lot in this place. Eating disorders, racism, harassment, assault, drugs . . ." He hands the scrap of paper to Pamela. ". . . even a bit of self-mutilation on a good day."

She smiles. A passing student notices the exchange. "Hot date, Mr. Monroe? Reckon you'll get your end in?"

Ben grins at Pamela. She notices a flicker of complicity fly between them. Or does she?

She strides buoyantly to the car park, absently notices the new scratch marks down one side of her car, and drives halfway to the Blue Mountains before realizing she's going in the wrong direction.

In her kitchen that evening, she dances wildly to her favorite feel-good music from her youth, singing along enthusiastically: "What I like about *you!* You hold me *tight!* . . ."

From her handbag she retrieves Ben's phone number and

anchors it with a magnet to her fridge, then stands back and stares at it proudly. A man's phone number. It stands out like a beacon among the collage of Pamela's adventures. Photos of her rock climbing in South America, parasailing in Bali, scuba-diving in the Red Sea, mountain-trekking in the Himalayas . . . One for every heartbreak. But right now Pamela feels as if she's on top of Everest. She can't remember the last time she met a man to whom she felt genuinely, unexpectedly attracted. She couldn't see whether he had "bastard" written on his forehead, so she'd better get Terri to check him out as soon as possible. She's begged Terri to warn her in advance next time. But she's certainly got a good feeling. She stares at his handwriting. Ben Monroe. She compulsively sounds out the unspeakable in her head. "Pamela Monroe." Not, of course, that she'd ever actually change her name if she got married . . . Oh, for Gods sake. She hits herself on the skull. "Idiot!"

The fridge is woefully empty, except for a couple of black-ened bananas, a row of low-fat soy-milk cartons, and half a loaf of bread. She grabs the last in the row of milk cartons and sniffs it. It barely passes the test, but she pours some into a bowl of breakfast cereal anyway, moving energetically to the music.

"Keep on whispering in my ear . . . tell me all the things . . ."

At the sound of the telephone she jumps, zapping off the CD-player. *Could it be him? No, don't be stupid, he doesn't have my number. Maybe he called work and Sally gave it to him, which she absolutely shouldn't have done—but she might have. . . .* She lets the phone ring twice more, then answers with anticipation. "Hello? . . . Who? . . . Oh, hi, Allen."

Aaarghh!

"Yes, actually, I am a bit busy. Next Sunday? . . . Uh, no,

sorry. Look, I'm pretty busy. I think I might be going away. . . . Yes, all right. I'll call you when I know what I'm doing. . . . Okay. Sorry. 'Bye."

She curses herself for being such a gutless wonder and takes another mouthful of breakfast cereal. The phone rings again. At the very least, it won't be Allen.

"Hello? . . . Oh, hi, Mum. . . . Yeah, I'm in the middle of dinner, but it doesn't matter. . . . Oh. . . . just steak and vegetables. How are you?"

She takes another mouthful of her dinner.

"Tonight? No, nothing. I've got work to do. . . . I do look after myself! I do get out! . . . I've seen people. Do you always have to do this? . . . I'm not being sensitive. . . . Mum, I have not chosen a solitary lifestyle."

She puts the milk back into the fridge, her mood altered for the worse, and as she closes the door she is faced with Ben's phone number.

A mess of garbled voices talk over one another. Pamela's cassette player struggles to digest the chewed tape that she has painstakingly rewound by hand. The result is not easy listening.

"I wannabee reech aaand sixessfoool . . ."

She fast-forwards, then rewinds again. Pressing Play, she is relieved to hear a slight improvement.

"I'm going to marry my hunky boyfriend, Jared, and have four kids."

She sits at her desk, typing as she listens, an open packet of Tim-Tams sitting next to her and half a biscuit sticking out of her mouth. Her study is lined with shelves crammed with

55

books and journals. The top of the filing cabinet is crowded with a collection of dust-covered trophies, and framed awards hang on the wall.

"Yeah, I want to get married and have a family and that, but like, not straightaway."

She takes a bite of Tim-Tam and surveys the bounty of her career: the trophies, the awards, and a framed newspaper clipping showing a much younger Pamela accepting a check as Cadet of the Year.

"But I don't reckon you should leave it too late. Like my auntie. You should see her. She's desperate."

"Yeah, you end up old and dried up and then no one wants you."

She presses Stop.

She sands a wooden door frame vigorously, the action producing an unbearable rasping noise that sets her teeth on edge. That's it. She throws down the sandpaper and clenches her fists in frustration.

Grabbing the phone, she runs into the kitchen and pulls Ben's number off the fridge. She takes a deep breath.

"Hello, Ben? Hi. it's Pamela Drury . . . the journalist . . . from this afternoon. Look, this might sound crazy . . ."

She squeezes her eyes shut, choosing her words carefully. "I mean . . . I don't normally do this type of . . . But I was wondering—I mean, just say if this is inappropriate—but I was wondering if . . . if . . . if . . . Oh, *fuck*."

She glowers at the phone. If only she had the guts to dial.

She rifles through her filing cabinet. "Come on, you've got to be in here somewhere."

Nothing. Fuming, she scans her shelves. Why does she always have to be in such a bloody mess? Her eyes alight on a corner of something peering out from under a pile of papers and she pounces, unearthing a folded tear sheet of her article "To Be or Not to Be: The Question of Teenage Suicide." She kisses it.

She grabs a fresh piece of paper, settles at her desk, and ponders the challenge at hand. What to say? How to start? "Dear Ben" is way too familiar. "Hi, there!" "Hi!" "Ben!" She opts for no greeting at all. Okay. Then what? "Please find enclosed . . . here is the article you said you wanted . . . I happened to find an extra copy . . . you said you were interested . . ."

Several sheets of paper later, she abandons the self-evident information and decides to concentrate on the hard stuff.

"I was wondering if you'd like to . . . Actually I do need to do some more research . . . I thought maybe over coffee . . ." Screaming, she screws up her latest effort and throws it across the room.

She beats herself up on the abdominal cruncher she bought off the television one night during a fit of insomnia. Why is she so pathetic? She squeezes her aching tummy muscles with a vengeance. Why can't she face the fear? She's intelligent and attractive, with a good job and a sense of humor. Plus, she's almost given up smoking. Granted, she doesn't cook, but these days you can buy really good-quality take-away. She's a good catch by anyone's standards, damn it! And if he isn't interested, then it doesn't mean she's worthless. He might be gay after all. In fact, he probably is gay. Almost certainly is. In which case he will make a very nice friend. She can introduce him to all her other gay friends.

Pamela runs to her desk to sustain the momentum.

Dear Ben,

I enjoyed meeting you today. Would you like to have coffee sometime? My number is 9836-1444, or call me at *Focal Point*.

Regards, Pamela Drury.

She types "Monroe" and presses Search. She knew the Internet would come in handy for something. Of course, if she hadn't used the phonebooks to support her desk, which lost a leg in the move . . . She balks at the number of entries, scrolling down the list in search of a match to the phone number she clutches in her hand. The numbers run together in a blur.

She finds it.

She slips the article and cover note into an envelope and seals it.

Ben Monroe
28 Paradise Avenue
Birchfield 2997

She looks at the letter with satisfaction. A flash of lightning floods the street and a crash of thunder rattles the windows. She sighs and readies for a storm.

Rain drips into an array of saucepans and Tupperware strategically placed throughout the apartment. Pamela swears for the umpteenth time that she will get the roof fixed, but she hates waiting for repairmen, and the fact is, she hasn't discovered any other use for the saucepans.

She searches her wallet for a postage stamp. Receipts, credit cards, cash . . . She empties out the entire contents and shakes her wallet vigorously. All she comes up with is a tattered Par Avion sticker.

She lies on the floor, legs propped up against the wall, and turns the letter over and over in her hands. The rain hits the saucepans. Plink . . . plink . . . plink. Like Chinese water torture.

The windshield wipers struggle to keep a patch of glass clear of water. The letter lays on the dashboard. She drives through the pouring rain while studying the street directory. What on earth is she doing on the road during such conditions? She can only conclude that she has graduated from clinical depression to some kind of obsessive-compulsive disorder. She slows down; the wipers are fighting a losing battle against the torrential rain. Disoriented, she strains to get her bearings. Then, spotting a street sign, she brakes. Paradise Avenue.

Through the rain, she scans the houses for numbers: 34 . . . 32 . . . 30. Number 28 turns out to be a block of flats, and she curses. Just her luck. She peers up through her windshield at the lit windows and the flickering televisions in the apartments. An elderly man closes his blinds; a middle-aged couple argues at the kitchen sink; a mother rocks her baby. No sign of a Student Crisis Counselor.

When the rain eases, she parks her car, grabs a plastic shopping bag off the backseat, wraps it over her head, and makes a dash for the row of letter boxes outside the front entrance. She scans the names: Cameron . . . Ogilvy . . . Haratzis . . . *Monroe.* The adrenaline starts pumping. She pushes the letter into the slot, but she can't let go of it. She bites her lip. It's not too late to go home and forget about the whole thing—*and feel even more pathetic and self-despising than ever.* In a turmoil of vacillation she stands there in the rain, then braces herself and lets go. The letter falls into the box in perfect synchronization with an enormous crack of thunder.

59

She runs through the teeming rain to the car, and as she opens the door her attention is caught by movement in the ground-floor flat. She freezes. It's him. She ducks behind the car and peeps over the hood so she can see straight into his kitchen, where he is cleaning up after dinner. Unaware of being observed, he energetically sings and wiggles as he throws rubbish in the bin, wipes the counter, and returns a book to a shelf bulging with what appear to be cookbooks.

Pamela swoons. *He cooks!*

Ben takes an opened bottle of wine from the bench, switches off the radio, and exits the kitchen.

Please, God, don't make him an alcoholic.

Pushing through the wet bushes, Pamela sneaks closer. It is pouring rain, and her sneakers sink into the muddy ground as she edges up to the window and peers in through a crack in the curtains. She can hear the strains of the television, but her view is obstructed. Crouching down, she makes her way along the window to the next crack in the curtains. Thunder rumbles as she peers in. Though there's movement in the room, she can't make out anything distinct. At that moment there's a flash of lightning and the rumble turns into a huge clap of thunder. She dodges from view, breathless.

As she sneaks another look, someone approaches the window. In a single movement the curtains are pulled open. Pamela ducks away, trips, and falls backward onto her bottom in the mud, looking up to see Ben framed in the window with a little girl on his shoulders, and a pretty woman with flame-red hair holding a toddler. The family tableau stands at the window, watching the lightning flash across the sky as the children squeal with delight.

Raindrops course down Pamela's face as she sits in the

mud. The drops pour down the windshield on her way home, but by then she can no longer tell if they are tears or rain or both.

Muddy and bedraggled, she rifles through the drawers of her dressing table, finding an asssortment of headache tablets, PMT tablets, malaria pills, contraceptive pills, multivitamins for stress, No-Doz, a packet of razor blades . . . She regards the razor blades for a moment, then winces at the idea.

Instead, she seizes a bottle of sleeping tablets and tips its contents into her hand. Five tablets. She stares doubtfully at them. It always seems to take more than that in the movies.

The rain shows no signs of letting up. The saucepans are full and water starts to overflow onto the livingroom floor. Pamela throws every towel in her possession at the sodden mess and takes refuge in the bathroom with her comfort kit. On the side of the bathtub, she props up a candle, a packet of cigarettes, an ashtray, and a bottle of gin. She struggles to light a cigarette with wet hands. In the background, Carole King assures her that she's got a friend.

Lying back and forcing her head under the water, she wonders how difficult it is to drown oneself in the bath. She counts to nineteen before surfacing, gasping like a drowned rat—or, more accurately, a drunken rat. She reaches for the bottle of gin and takes a swig, then closes her damp fingers around the cigarette and drags deeply.

"When the sky above you grows dark and full of clouds . . ."

She sniffs. It's looking pretty bloody dark and cloudy right now. No, this one didn't have "bastard" stamped on him. He had "married bastard" printed from ear to ear, didn't he? She should have known. And why? Because there are no single men left. She's thrown away the only man that God meant her to marry, and now it's too late. *There must be approximately five good single men left in the metropolitan area, and fifty thousand fantastic women; so the guys have the pick of the crop, and that sure counts me out. All they want is a spunky little wife to look after them. Hell, who in their right mind wouldn't?* . . . Even she's tired of eating take-away and squeezing her own orange juice. Tired. Tired. Tired.

As she blows smoke rings into the suds, she notices the hair dryer lying on top of the toilet and reaches for it, curling her wet fingers around the handle and bringing it to her head, gun-style. Closing her eyes, she squeezes the "trigger," producing a noisy blast of hot air to her temple. Then she opens her mouth wide and points the "gun" into her mouth, all the time with slow, deliberate contemplation. She closes her eyes, pulls the trigger, and recoils at the burst of hot air shooting into her mouth.

"Winter, spring, summer, or fa-all, all you have to do is ca-all . . ."

She studies the dryer in her wet hand, aware of its lethal potential. She lowers it toward the surface of the water, watching the hot air part the soap bubbles before it. As if compelled by an inner force, she brings the dryer closer to the water. Very, very slowly. Closer, closer, until there is an infinitesimal space between the tip of the dryer and the surface of the water.

The water quivers. The air is tense. At that moment Carole King cuts off abruptly, and the overhead light goes out.

Silence. The candle flickers, casting an eerie light over the room. Pamela stands and peers through the bars of the small bathroom window to the dark night and torrential rain. The streetlights are out. A power failure. Typical. Can't even manage to off herself. Still clutching the hair dryer, she looks at it sourly and pulls the trigger. A pathetic click. She drops the dryer into the bath. Plop. Splash. It sinks to her feet.

Pamela stares at the dryer through the soapy water. What is it that makes her so hopeless? Why can't she just bow out gracefully? "Thanks for the good times, God. Sorry I stared a gift man in the mouth, and cheerio!"

The bathroom is lit up by a flash of lightning. Suddenly overcome with a burst of cowardice, Pamela leaps out of the bath. She catches her leg on the side of the tub and hits the floor with a thud.

"Shit!"

She lies on her bed, alone in the darkness, while Kanga watches from her bedside table. Her hair's still damp and she's pulled her bathrobe half over her. Through a haze of drunken misery, she listens to the sound of rain running through the outside drains. City sounds and distant laughter filter into the room. A party of late-night revelers shouts noisy good-byes, slams car doors, and roars off into the distance.

The bed starts to rotate slowly, and the ceiling swirls menacingly. She curls up, pulls the toy kangaroo to her, and hugs it tightly.

Happy Happy Happy 5

The sun streams in through the bathroom window and falls across Pamela, who lies slumped against the toilet bowl, asleep. When the telephone rings she winces at the piercing noise. The answering machine cuts in.

"Pam . . . Max. You're not here, so I'm assuming you're there. Will you pick up, then? . . . All right, don't. Just get that bloody article on girls finished, or you'll never work in this town again."

She groans and scrapes herself off the bathroom floor. Shading her eyes from the sunlight, she steps into the shower and turns it on full force. Then she remembers to take off her bathrobe.

An hour later, hiding behind sunglasses and a broad-brimmed hat, Pamela seeks refuge under an umbrella at a side-walk table at La Fontana. She unfolds her newspaper and scans the headlines. A fizzing glass of Alka-Seltzer arrives under her nose.

"Get that into you. You look like death. Not even warmed up."

She smiles weakly. "Thanks, Charlie."

Charlie shakes his head. "You gotta look after yourself, Pamela."

"Yeah, yeah, I know."

She downs the Alka-Seltzer in one gulp. She's often wondered what it is about bubbles that is supposed to do you good. How can fizz settle your stomach when it's not settled itself? She remembers how her mother used to ply her with lemonade whenever she came down with a "bug." She suspects it will take more than fizz today to bring her around and wonders if she should line her stomach with some breakfast. She picks up the menu and contemplates a ham-and-cheese focaccia. Her stomach answers for her.

"Charlie, could I have a large black coffee, please? And a lemonade."

He shakes his head in disapproval.

She turns to the world news. But she can't seem to face any tragedy other than her own and gives up on the paper to watch a young mother at the next table breast-feeding her infant. She remembers reading that the experience of breast-feeding can rival that of sexual euphoria. The mother smiles at her. Pamela looks away, only to be faced with a passionate young couple spoon-feeding each other the froth off their cappuccinos in a public display of unbridled lust.

Desperate for distraction, she goes through Charlie's tattered collection of free reading, pulling out an old copy of *Now Woman*, a glossy that she would normally avoid at all costs. She likens glossies to junk food—they may have a certain appeal, but you always feel ill after consuming them. Today she suc-cumbs. After all, she already feels ill. She flips it open and wonders if it is a special kick-Pamela-when-she's-down issue: "Single, Successful, and Stressed Out—Career Girls Tell All"; "*Your* Biological Clock—Does It Read Three Minutes to Mid-night?"; "Straight Available Men—What Are Your Chances of Finding One?"

She feels the tears begin to well up and stuffs the magazine back into the rack, leaves a handful of money by the cash reg-ister, and flees. Charlie calls after her, coffee in hand, but she keeps running.

Safely around the corner, she slows down to a walk and blows her nose. *Pull yourself together: go back to the flat and finish your article.* But she just can't face it. Maybe she should take herself to the movies. Get her mind off things. But she hates ac-tion films, and right now she couldn't stand a romance, either. And anyway, the thought of buying a lone ticket is too much. So she just keeps walking, in the hopes of walking it off. She doesn't care where she is going as long as the blackness doesn't follow her. That dreadful, aching blackness.

It is her feet that are aching two hours later when she finds herself at a busy intersection somewhere in the city, looking for a place to sit down. The Don't Walk sign is flashing. She bangs the pedestrian button four times, even though she knows it has already been pressed.

"Excuse me."

A skinny, pockmarked young man with a clipboard smiles at her. Pamela inwardly groans.

"I'm conducting a survey. Do you have a moment?"

She turns away, willing him to evaporate.

"It doesn't take long."

She looks up impatiently at the crossing sign.

"Great! Now, do you live in the city center vicinity?"

She reluctantly answers, "Yes."

"And are you employed?"

"Yes."

"Which age group describes you? Eighteen to twenty-five, twenty-five to thirty, thirty to thirty-five—?"

"Stop!"

The young man smiles knowingly and checks a box. "Do you consider yourself to be happy?"

Pamela frowns. "Pardon?"

He clears his throat. "Do you have faith in our Lord Jesus Christ?"

Her face sets. "As a matter of fact, I am happy. See?" She grins like an idiot. "Happy happy happy! Probably a lot happier than you, you patronizing little . . . prick. Now piss off!"

She turns sharply and steps off the curb. A car horn sounds and brakes screech to a halt. Her head hits the curb with a thud. As she lies on the road, stunned, the smell of burned rubber floats in the air. A car door opens and shuts and someone runs toward her.

"Oh, my God, are you all right? I didn't see you. You came out of nowhere! Are you all right? Are you hurt? Should I call an ambulance?"

"No, no, I think I'm all right. I'm fine."

Shaken, Pamela gingerly brushes herself off and tries to get up, but her body won't cooperate.

"Are you sure you're all right?"

She turns toward the voice. Her vision is blurred and she struggles to focus on the woman leaning over her. The silver spots that cloud her view start to clear and her eyes lock on to a face. She blinks, confused. She recognizes the face. It is her own. Apart from a different hairstyle, she could be looking at . . . herself. The woman is also struck by the uncanny resemblance. The two gape at each other, nonplussed.

The woman tries to speak. "You just stepped out . . . I didn't see you . . . I'm sorry . . . I was—"

Pamela answers automatically. "No . . . no . . . not your fault. I wasn't—"

"But I should have seen you."

The two women stare at each other.

Pamela is confounded. "Actually, I'm feeling a bit . . . Do you think you could help me up?"

The woman guides her into the passenger's seat of a late-model four-wheel drive.

"I . . . I think I should take you to a doctor. You might have a concussion."

Pamela can't take her eyes off the woman. "No, I don't think so . . . I don't think a concussion feels like this."

The woman looks around nervously. "Well, let me take you home. Is there someone there to look after you? Do you live around here?"

Pamela shakes her head. "No—I mean, yes, I live around here . . . somewhere. And no, there's no one there."

The woman frowns. "I don't think I should leave you here on the street. You've had a nasty shock."

Pamela shivers. Maybe it is shock. She can't be sure. After all, she's only ever seen herself in the mirror and in photos, so she doesn't know exactly how she looks in three dimensions, but this person certainly seems to be a pretty good facsimile. "Have . . . have you noticed . . . you look just like me?"

The woman nods nervously. "They do say there are only a certain number of types of people in the world. But it's not every day that you run over one of your own type!" She tries to smile to reassure herself as much as Pamela.

Another shiver runs down Pamela's spine. "But you've got my voice too." At that thought, her brain short-circuits and she passes out.

When she comes to, it's to the sound of birds singing. She opens her eyes onto a beautiful garden, full of roses in bloom, Chilean jasmine and crimson bougainvillea. A heavenly scent is in the air. She realizes she is still in the passenger's seat of the four-wheel-drive, which has just pulled up in the driveway of a tastefully renovated Victorian house. Pamela's look-alike pulls the keys from the ignition and takes off her seat belt. She leans over to Pamela and unbuckles her belt for her.

"Let's go in and have a cup of coffee. You can rest here—till you feel better."

Pamela's head aches. "I'm dead, aren't I? You must be my guardian angel. In the form of . . . me. So that you don't scare me. Like in that film with Jodie Foster. Except that was an alien in the form of her father. Are you an alien or an angel?"

The woman smiles uncertainly. "I'm not aware of being either."

Pamela stares at her, transfixed. She can see the woman is just as unnerved as she is. "I hope I'm not dead. This is going to make one hell of an article."

At that moment, an exuberant golden retriever leaps up to the passenger's window and slobbers on the glass. Pamela jumps with fright. Brandy looks at her and tilts his head inquisitively.

She hovers on the veranda while the front door is being un-
locked and the alarm system is switched off. She's fascinated by
the garden, which somehow reminds her of her childhood. Her
mother has always been a mad gardener, the creator of a half-
tamed world of color and perfume and light and shade. As a
child, Pamela used to spend hours collecting ladybirds and
Christmas beetles, while Mum weeded and potted and pruned
her precious climbing roses. Dad would mow the lawn on Sunday mornings, but the garden was Mum's domain. She called it
her one creative outlet after sacrificing the rest of her life. But
they'd moved into the unit and her back was giving out on her,
she could manage only a tiny walled courtyard, but she still
worked wonders with it and referred to it as her secret garden. Pamela fancied that she had inherited her mother's green
thumb, if only she had a garden in which to try it out. She'd always dreamed of the day she could afford to buy a real house
and create her own secret garden. But with the way real estate
was these days, she knew she'd never do it on a single income.

The uncanny thing is that this garden looks just like the
garden of her dreams, the garden she's always wanted to have,
the roses and jasmine and wisteria and bougainvillea, down to
the border of hyacinths and jonquils lining the path.

"The kitchen's through here."

Pamela starts at the sound of her own voice, marveling at
the exact simulation.

She enters an average family kitchen in mild disarray, with
a jumble of children's paintings on the cupboards and fridge
door. The walls are a warm yellow, the woodwork blue. The
friendliness embraces her as she stares at a colorful painting of
Mummy and Daddy.

Her hostess registers her curiosity. "You should've seen the

71

place when we bought it. A complete dump." Talking quickly, she fills the kettle and plugs it in. "Actually, I think it was the most fun we've had together. I painted, while my husband did the sanding. Can't stand sanding. Something about the noise, you know? Like fingernails running down a blackboard."

Pamela nods, knowing too well. She watches the alien busy herself with the coffee. She takes in the corduroy pants, T-shirt, denim overshirt, and the long hair scooped up into a soft, messy bun, flecked with gray. Pamela remembers wearing her hair like that years ago. That's what it would look like now if she just let it go. Instead, she sports a short, modern cut, colored to a sort of burgundy to extinguish any signs of gray.

She peels off her leather jacket and hangs it on the back of a kitchen stool, eyes still riveted to the woman who looks just like her. It is the weirdest sensation, watching her go to the fridge and get the milk out. Even the mannerisms are familiar. She shivers and catches the woman sneaking a glance at her.

"Why don't you go and sit in the lounge? You don't look so good."

Unlike Pamela's own disaster area of a living room, everything here is in order. Her eyes go to a box of children's toys in one corner, then to a photo gallery on the wall. She's drawn to a gold-framed wedding photo. A classic white wedding with a glowing bride and handsome groom posing on the steps of St. John's. Perfectly normal, except upon closer inspection the bride looks just like Pamela in her early twenties, and the groom—"Robert Dickson!"

She's spellbound. "But I turned him down! I said no."

"I didn't."

The woman steps up next to Pamela as Pamela feels her head start to hurt again.

"So you're . . . really me? Pamela Drury?"

The woman half nods, half shakes her head.

"Pamela . . . Dickson."

Pamela Drury tries to comprehend. She turns back to the gallery. Underneath the wedding picture is a series of photos: Robert holding Pamela upside down on a tropical beach; pregnant Pamela in Robert's arms; a proud Pamela and Robert with a newborn baby; Robert with a girl toddler astride his shoulders, while Pamela nurses another newborn baby; Pamela and Robert with a young girl, a boy, and yet another newborn baby.

"Stacy's twelve and a half. Douglas is ten. That was going to be it. And then came Rupert. He was a . . . diaphragm baby."

Convinced she is losing her mind, Pamela is scarcely able to process this information. She knows for a fact she never married Robert Dickson, and she knows she hasn't shared a life with him. She can account for every moment since the proposal, and he sure as hell wasn't there. And yet, in a surreal way, these photos look so normal, so perfect. There she is, in the arms of the love of her life, in the midst of a growing family. As she stares at the pictures, they seem to form a jigsaw, completed by a long-lost piece of herself.

When she had imagined her dream life with Robert in moments of forlorn reverie, she had always embellished it with a little girl and a boy. The girl she would indeed have named Stacy, after the tomboy rebel in one of her favorite girlhood novels. And Douglas was Pamela's father's name. She squints at the baby boy. Rupert. She turns up her nose in distaste. A truly dreadful choice, but somehow familiar . . .

"*Rupert?*"

The other Pamela nods apologetically. "I know, I know. Rob's—"

"—great-grandfather." Pamela stifles a laugh. "Whoa!"

Pamela watches Pamela Dickson pour the coffee. For every flash of comprehension, she feels a tightening knot in her stomach. They must be the same people, and yet they can't be. Could Robert's proposal have been the defining moment in both their lives? Were they like spiritual Siamese twins, joined at birth and separated by a crucial decision? Pamela catches herself. Of course not. She's got to be in the middle of an incredibly vivid dream, that's all. It must have been something she ate. The other Pamela is simply a figment of her overwrought subconscious. Unless, of course, *she's* a figment of the other Pamela's . . . No, she can't go there. Pamela wonders whether she should pinch herself. But *which* self? One of them must be an impostor, but the other Pamela is playing her role to the hilt.

"Earliest memory?"

Pamela Dickson looks at her blankly. "What?"

"What's your earliest memory?"

She racks her brain. "God . . . I don't think I've got one." Pamela grins triumphantly. Hail the impostor! Pamela Dickson regards her curiously.

"Have you?"

Pamela's moment of triumph fades as she thinks. She bites her lip.

"I'm sure I used to be able to remember back to when I was two. But I can't anymore. I've got a terrible memory these days."

"Me, too. I thought it was hormonal. You know—the kids."

"Really? I thought it was the alcohol and cigarettes. What about kindergarten?"

"Tommy Higginbothom throwing up on me!"

Pamela thumps the countertop. "Yes! I still can't stand the smell of egg mayonnaise!"

"Let alone eat it!"

They grimace at the memory.

Pamela Dickson hands Pamela her coffee. They both take a sip simultaneously. Each Pamela cannot take her eyes off the other. They smile awkwardly.

"First period."

Struck by the question, Pamela Dickson furrows her brow. "Ooh . . . it was a Saturday morning. Summer. I was supposed to be meeting the others at the beach. I was only . . . what— twelve? Thought it was the end of the world. Mum—"

Pamela takes over. "Caught me trying to burn my underpants in the incinerator. What was it she said? . . ."

"You should be pleased—"

"—that you're becoming a woman!"

Pamela looks at her other self, utterly aghast. "This is the most—"

"—incredible dream I've ever had."

They stare at each other, awestruck.

"Remember school? Philip—"

"O'Rourke! Sticking his tongue down my throat!"

"And Sebastian—"

"You mean 'Kevin'!"

They hoot with laughter.

"What about that disgusting math exam that I cheated on?"

"I never told a soul, you know."

"Me, either."

Pamela smiles, trawling through the years.

"Starting uni. Moving out . . ."

"Freedom!"

"Sex!"

Pamela grins. "Robert."

Pamela Dickson smiles. "The Deadbeats!"

"Mmm. Falling in love."

Pamela screws up her nose. "That awful moldy—"

"—futon!"

Pamela Dickson says wistfully, "Remember sleeping naked on the back lawn that night?"

Pamela nods. "God, summers were hot in those days."

"Or what about that storm? During the reception. The poor garden. Poor Mum! She was a wreck!"

"Yeah . . ."

They shake their heads at the memories. Pamela's brow furrows. "What reception?"

Then she realizes.

Pamela Dickson drags out a box of photo albums. She pulls out the oldest album and flips it open. Pamela pales as she recognizes it as exactly the same album she keeps in a box in her study—down to the cut-out palomino mare and foal she glued on the front when she was eleven. This is her history. No, it is a shared history. How can it be that every single event in her life, every occasion, momentous and trivial, lives in the other Pamela's memory as strongly as in her own? Up until a point, that is. For Pamela Dickson opens up another album. An album of unshared memories: the wedding at St. John's, the reception ruined by the storm. Pamela pores hungrily over the unfamiliar photos.

"That was just after I had Stacy. God, I look so young. Oh my God, don't ever go camping in the rain with two small children. . . . That's a nice one. We'd just got Brandy."

At the sound of his name, Brandy wags his tail excitedly and rubs against his mistress, who pats him lovingly, pointing to another photo. "Douglas's fifth birthday party."

"He's so *cute*. He looks just like a baby Robert!"

"Cute? That was just after he'd been expelled from kindergarten for biting off Jessica Humphrey's ear—well, not right off . . ." She leans over the album to the photo of Douglas grinning cheekily. A tear splashes on the page. She looks to Pamela in surprise and snaps the album shut. "Enough of that. Why don't you tell me about all the exciting things in your life? You must have done so much!"

Pamela starts sobbing. Pamela Dickson stares at her. Unsure of what to do, she tentatively puts a hand on Pamela's heaving shoulder. Both of them are acutely aware that this is the first time they have touched. Each notes that the other certainly feels like flesh and blood.

Pamela tries to wipe away her tears. "I guess you don't smoke?"

Pamela Dickson shakes her head apologetically. "Gave it up years ago. Can't with a family, you know."

Pamela nods and blows her nose. There's a noise outside and Brandy starts barking noisily. Pamela Dickson looks at the clock and turns to Pamela, alarmed. "The kids! From school!"

She grabs Pamela's leather jacket off the chair and holds it out to her. "Quick!"

Pamela hesitates. "Maybe I'm invisible!"

At that moment, Douglas, a ten-year-old crew cut on Rollerblades, bursts through the door and dumps his backpack on the kitchen floor with a thud. He blades straight to the fridge without so much as glancing at Pamela. It occurs to her that she is indeed invisible. She tentatively tests this theory by waving at him. He doesn't respond. She tries more emphatic gestures. Douglas still doesn't respond. Pamela is delighted. As she turns to Pamela Dickson, she is struck by the weirdest sensation, as if she's experiencing déjà vu from somebody else's perspective. She waves at Douglas again. She *is* invisible! Delighted, she turns once more to Pamela Dickson. But Pamela Dickson is not there.

Stacy enters. She's a twelve-year-old in baggy grunge attire with a mass of carefully unkempt hair streaked fluoro-pink. She stops short. "God, what've you done to your hair?"

Pamela is taken aback. Douglas still has his head in the fridge. He grabs a loaf of bread and proceeds to prepare a stack of sandwiches. He leaves a mess on the counter, and exits through the back door, while Stacy pours herself a drink and goes into the living room. Pamela's left standing in the middle of the kitchen in a state of shock. She feels a tugging at her shirt and looks down.

"Can I have some juice?"

An angelic-looking four-year-old with golden blond hair and blue eyes gazes up at her. He is clutching a well-worn but unmistakably familiar toy kangaroo; once white, now gray.

Pamela goes to the fridge. Finding a row of fruit-juice boxes, she hands one to Rupert, who promptly hands it back to her. "You do it."

Pamela is at a loss.

". . . Please."

Realizing her mistake, she pulls the straw from its plastic seal, punctures the box, and hands it back to Rupert. As he takes it, he gazes steadily at her. As if he knows.

Sucking noisily on the straw, he disappears down the hallway, leaving Pamela to herself. Rattled, she wheels around and calls in an urgent whisper. "Pamela . . . Pamela!"

Nothing. Just a whimper. Pamela turns. Brandy is lying on the floor. Looking at her with big sad eyes, he raises his head high and lets out a mournful cry. Pamela shivers and reaches for her leather jacket. It's not there.

Two Boys
and a Girl

6

Stacy is lying on the couch in front of the television as Pamela peers around the doorway and watches her. She could be looking at herself at that age, except for the pink-streaked hair and the glitter nail polish. To think of her genes running around in someone else's body! She struggles to come to terms with the nature of their connection.

Stacy senses she is being watched. "*What?*"

Pamela jumps. "Uh . . . nothing . . . I was just wondering . . . what you are watching?"

Stacy groans and raises her eyes to the ceiling. "Get a life!" She rolls off the couch, switches off the television, and storms out of the room, slamming her bedroom door behind her, while Pamela stares after her.

Startled by the sound of frantic barking, she goes to the

window. Outside, Douglas is using octopus straps to tie Rupert to a skateboard. Brandy races around the boys in agitation.

Douglas launches the skateboard, complete with hostage, down the driveway. It gathers speed rapidly, with Brandy chasing after it and barking noisily. Rupert, a live torpedo, is hurtling toward the road. At the bottom of the driveway the skateboard skews to the side and crashes on the grass.

Douglas whoops and rollerblades to the wreckage. "Impact diabolical!"

He unstraps Rupert, who appears a little stunned but unhurt. Pamela arrives on the scene. Seeing Pamela, Douglas reddens guiltily, his tone aggressive.

"He's all right! He wanted to do it!"

She looks to Rupert, who is struggling free of the octopus strap. "Are you all right?"

Rupert looks to Douglas, then nods his head. Pamela doesn't know what to say. If she had kids, she'd never let them do that sort of thing. "Well, maybe you should use a helmet next time. You've got a helmet, haven't you?"

Douglas looks at Pamela, astonished.

She circles the family car, which is still parked in the driveway. Wherever Pamela Dickson has got to, it wasn't by normal means. She must be around here somewhere. Pamela tries to remain calm in the face of complete and utter incomprehension. She'll turn up. She has to. She's just giving her a chance to see the kids, that's all. There's probably some logic to this dream that says they can't be in the presence of the children together. If it is a dream. She racks her brain to fathom at what point she could have fallen asleep. Hitting a blank, she decides to go back into the kitchen and wait there for Pamela Dickson.

Deafening music blares from Stacy's bedroom. In the livingroom, Douglas commands a set of video-game controls. Rupert is sitting with him on the couch, hugging Kanga and sucking his thumb. Both sets of eyes are riveted to the television screen as Douglas obliterates the deadly enemy.

The nightmarish blend of rock music and violent video games swirls around Pamela as she sits numbly at the kitchen counter. She frantically empties the contents of Pamela Dickson's bag: lipstick, tissues, hair clips, supermarket vouchers, credit cards, checkbook, driver's license. She stares at the photo ID. There she is. Pamela Dickson. She stares at the evidence of her other self. The hairs on the back of her neck are working overtime, and her head is still hurting. She looks to Brandy, who is watching her closely, and she reaches out to pat him. His lip curls and he snarls menacingly. Startled, Pamela pulls back her hand.

Douglas appears grumpily at the doorway. "What's for tea?"

She tries to find her way around the unfamiliar kitchen, opening every single cupboard and drawer, not at all sure of what she is looking for. Who is she kidding anyway? She can't cook. She is, however, beginning to feel hungry herself, and she realizes that she hasn't eaten anything since . . . since before . . . for a long time. She searches for a Cuisine Courier menu. Without success.

She hovers at the doorway of the living room. "How about eggs on toast?"

Douglas turns up his nose and sticks his tongue out, while Rupert merely frowns.

She retreats to the kitchen, feeling like the victim of an extremely elaborate practical joke. Do they still make *Candid Camera*? she wonders. She decides not to break down sobbing, just in case. She won't give them the satisfaction. Shaking her-

83

self out of that line of thinking and concluding that she's losing her mind, she opens the freezer. It is packed with frozen pizzas; she unwraps one and heats it up in the oven.

She cuts up the pizza and hands the slices around. Douglas pokes at his burned slice with distaste, while Brandy hovers next to him, drooling excessively.

Douglas takes a bite. "Do you know what I want to have?" he asks aggressively, his mouth full of pizza.

Stacy sighs. "Scintillating conversation?"

He ignores the jab. "Give up? A broken leg! That'd be so cool."

"I'll give you one if you like."

Douglas sticks out his pizza-laden tongue at her. "With a plaster cast. That everybody can sign all over."

Pamela's attention is fixed on the empty seat opposite her. It hasn't escaped her attention that there is one thing missing from this scenario. Robert Dickson. Where is he? She can't very well ask the children. They haven't mentioned him, nor do they seem upset by his absence. *Maybe he's working late. Maybe he always works late. Maybe none of this really exists anyway.*

"Where was it? Mum, what was it called? *Mum!*"

Pamela doesn't realize that she is being addressed, and Stacy puts Douglas out of his misery. "Katoomba."

Douglas nods. "Or a broken arm. My right arm, so I couldn't write. Wouldn't have to do schoolwork. It'd be so tough. To go to hospital and everything. They reckon you have to go to the toilet in your bed. Is that true, Mum?"

Pamela turns to Douglas. He seems so familiar. . . . The nose, the eyes, the hairline, the funny way he eats his pizza . . . Just like a miniature version of Robert, only horrid.

"Mum? Is it true? Is it true? *Mum!*"

She shivers, snapping out of her reverie. "Hmm? What?"

"In hospital. What's it like? Do they stick tubes up you?"

She shakes her head. "I don't know. I've never been in hospital."

Douglas raises his eyes to the ceiling. "You have so! Three times. For Stacy, me, and Rupert. Dumbhead!"

Stacy takes another piece of pizza and throws Douglas a derisive glance. "That wasn't a hospital. It was a birthing center. Dumbhead." She smirks smugly and awaits her mother's confirmation. Pamela can only nod weakly.

While Stacy and Douglas watch *X-Files,* Rupert plays with his Lego blocks on the floor. He yawns and rubs his eyes.

Brandy sits in the kitchen, whining mournfully. Pamela turns her back to the dog and hastily dials the kitchen phone. She crouches down, under the kitchen counter.

"Unfortunately, the number you have dialed is incomplete or incorrect. Please check the number and try again. Unfortunately, the number . . ."

Rattled, she hangs up and dials Information. She speaks in a low voice. "Drury. Initial P. . . . No—P. For . . . Peculiar. Barnes Avenue."

Brandy continues to whine and Pamela glares at him. "Shh! . . . Sorry? . . . None? . . . Are you sure? . . . *None?* . . . Well, could you try ag——"

The operator hangs up. Unnerved, she considers the options. One: She's dreaming. Two: She's dead. Three: She's having a nervous breakdown. Four: She's at a party and someone's spiked her drink. She quite likes the last option. The only thing is, she can't remember the last time she went to a party, having sworn off them as an extremely depressing and futile method of meeting men.

85

She dials another number. When it rings at the other end, she closes her eyes and prays. "Come on, Terri, be there." Brandy starts barking. "Shut up!"

She notices Rupert standing in the doorway gazing solemnly at her as she huddles under the kitchen counter. "He hasn't been fed."

Defeated, she hangs up the unanswered phone.

In the pantry she eventually finds a can of Chum. Recoiling at the repulsive smell that hits her in the face when she opens it, she searches the cupboards for a dog plate, wondering where people who keep dogs keep the dog plates. In the end she places a Bunnikins baby bowl on the back step, piled high with dog food. "There you are. That should shut you up."

But Brandy won't come near her. He keeps his distance, growling suspiciously.

"What do you think? I've poisoned it?"

He barks sharply and she shrugs.

"Well, it's up to you. It's either that or frozen pizza."

She goes back into the house, banging the door shut behind her. From inside she watches as Brandy cautiously approaches the plate, gives the food a lick, then proceeds to wolf it down.

She slides down the door, curls up into a ball on the floor, and starts rocking back and forth, singing softly, "Winter, spring, summer, or fa-all, all you have to do is ca-all . . ."

She paces the hallway, the day's events replaying over and over in her head. She can't make sense of it all, for the pure and simple reason that it doesn't make sense, so it's very hard to come up with any kind of strategy for coping. What she needs is a plan. She needs a plan for extraordinary circumstances. Like plane-crash victims who are stuck out in the wilderness with no food and water, or people whose camper vans break down in the middle of the Nullarbor Plain in hundred-degree heat, with only the contents of their radiators to drink. She once saw a television program about people who had survived such traumas and what they had in common. First, they all had unshakable faith that they would survive. Second, they all stayed with their vehicles. Unfortunately, Pamela can't relate to the first response. She knows she'd be the one to give up hope by the end of day one, expire on day two, and end up being eaten by the other passengers when the rations ran out on day three. That left staying with the vehicle.

She peers into the living room, where Stacy and Douglas are now watching an extremely violent police show. Cars career through shop windows, shots are fired, heads are bashed, obscene language spews forth. Douglas yawns. She notices Rupert, fast asleep on the floor among his toys. She grimaces guiltily, remembering the award-winning article she wrote about the effects of television violence on children under five. She goes to him and tries to pick him up. He's deadweight and she can feel her back go. "Shit!" Her chiropractor told her not to lift anything heavy.

Awkwardly, she lugs the sleeping child down the hallway. Not knowing where she is going, she tentatively pushes open a door that has a sign on it reading "Keep Out." Bingo. She enters what is unmistakably a boys' bedroom, chooses the bed with a Sesame Street duvet and gingerly puts Rupert down. She stands back, wondering what to do next. Then, attempting to undress him, she succeeds in nearly decapitating him with his sweater. Sighing, she gives up on the clothes and simply pulls the duvet out from under him and covers him. Gazing at the sleeping boy in wonder, she picks Kanga up off the floor, noting the ripped

pouch and the loss of the baby joey. The fur is matted and there
is a radiator burn across its face. She stares into the one remaining glass eye. It stares back knowingly.

Pamela now scans the hallway and peers into the next
room.

"What are you doing?"

She jumps and turns to face Stacy. "Nothing. I was . . ."

Stacy pushes past her and goes into her room, emerging
seconds later with a large tape dispenser, which she hands de-
fensively to Pamela. "I was going to put it back!"

Pamela clutches the tape dispenser uncertainly, then backs
off and turns away while Stacy eyes her curiously.

"Are you all right?"

"What? Yes! No. Actually . . . I . . . I . . ." She yearns to
confide in someone. "I think I'm . . . I think I'm going . . ."

Stacy frowns at her and watches Pamela biting her lip.

". . . to bed."

Bracing herself, she looks left, then right, down the hallway.
Where the hell is her bedroom? She takes a guess and goes left.

Stacy watches after her. "Mum?"

Pamela freezes. How to explain that she doesn't know
where her own bedroom is? She turns slowly.

"If you haven't got your periods yet, do you have to use a
condom when you have sex?"

In the bedroom Pamela closes her eyes and bangs her head
against the wall. "Time to wake up. Pamela! Come on. Wake
up. You've got a deadline, for God's sake. Wake up!" God, how
she hates the kind of dream that you can't wake yourself out of.
She bangs her head again. The thumping on the wall results in
the wardrobe door swinging open with an eerie creak.

Rubbing her bruised head, she stares at the wardrobe. To

her astonishment, she recognizes it as the wardrobe she'd bought for 99 Edith Road. Except, of course, that its doors are attached, and it is not covered in five layers of crappy paint. It has been meticulously restored and stands with an impressive dignity in a corner. Trust Pamela Dickson to be able to run a house and a family, *and* have time for quality refurbishment.

She is drawn to the wardrobe. Of course, the wardrobe! Her heart beats fast as she gently parts the clothes and climbs in, the door closing with a creak behind her. Inside, it's totally dark. She pushes through the clothes, through the winter coats, breathing in the smell of mothballs . . . and hits the back of the wardrobe.

Disheartened, she stumbles back into the room and bangs the wardrobe door shut, catching her reflection in the mirror. She scrutinizes herself and is struck by an unsettling realization. "You're not asleep, are you?"

Outside a storm brews. Thunder rumbles and sheet lightning dances in the sky. She dials the bedside telephone and starts pacing.

"Please be there please be there please be there please be— *Mum!* Thank God! Mum, I think I'm going . . . What? Yeah, sorry, I know it's a bit late, but . . . I didn't mean to wake you, but I . . . What? The what?"

She feels her stomach turn to stone and her voice cracks.

"Oh . . . No. Nothing wrong . . . They're fine. The kids are fine. No, no . . . It's nothing really. I . . . er . . . had a nightmare. . . . Sorry, I didn't mean to wake you."

She sinks heavily onto the bed, staring at the framed photo of a smiling Robert and Pamela on the bedside table. Next to the photo lays a pair of cuff links and a half-empty bottle of aftershave. She picks up the cuff links and holds them in the palm of her hand, then takes the aftershave and sprays a puff into the air. She closes her eyes, breathing in the aroma. Her body reels at the whoosh of sensation from the past. Robert Dickson. Where is he?

The rain starts in a sudden downpour. A drop of water hits her face. She looks up to the ceiling and groans. Is she destined to be plagued by leaking ceilings? After fetching a saucepan from the kitchen, she positions it under the leak. Then she curls up on the bed beside the saucepan, hugs a pillow to her, and shuts her eyes tight. "I deserve the best and I accept the best. I deserve the best and I accept the best."

She awakens groggily. The early morning chorus filters in through the open window and the sun is low as she experiences a cloudy moment of not knowing where the hell she is. She vaguely remembers having one mother of a dream. She tries to blink the fuzziness away. It refuses to go. She rubs her eyes and focuses on a giant bumblebee looming down at her. Then she screams.

Douglas stares at his mother. She is lying in the fetal position, on one side of the bed, on top of the duvet, fully clothed, next to a saucepan. Dressed for football, in bold yellow-and-black stripes, Douglas taps his football boot impatiently on the floor. "Come on or I'll be late!"

Splashing cold water on her face, she stares at herself in the mirror of the en-suite bathroom, then pulls down her pants and sinks onto the toilet seat, taking a moment to collect what residue of wits she has left. But it is difficult to concentrate. Douglas waits in the car, pounding on the horn in an unrelenting assault of neighborhood-disturbing noise. She looks at her watch. It is seven-thirty A.M.

After wiping the dew off the windshield, she climbs into the four-wheel-drive and slams the door, noting the revolting cold smell of baby vomit that lingers in the upholstery. She takes her time putting her seat belt on and checks the mirrors. She's never driven anything this big before—the world outside looks so low and far away.

Douglas wiggles anxiously in the passenger's seat. "Come on! Let's go!"

Tentatively, she backs down the driveway and onto the street in a jerky fashion. She has absolutely no idea of her destination. She has absolutely no idea where she is, and absolutely nothing looks at all familiar. She guesses that they are way out in the northern suburbs somewhere, but she can't be sure, and she has a sudden vivid memory of playing Pin the Tail on the Donkey at Belinda Burton's eighth birthday party. She went last. The other children blindfolded her and spun her around and around, and then the birthday cake came out and they all ran off and left Pamela staggering in the dark, a cardboard tail in her hand.

She takes a stab at a left turn. Douglas clucks his tongue ill-temperedly. "What are you doing? Dad never goes this way."

She winces. "Doesn't he? Well, which way does he go?"

Douglas grunts impatiently. "The other way, dummy."

She makes a U-turn, but not without hitting the curb and crunching the gears.

Douglas makes a face. "What are you doing?"

Navigating uncertainly, she is guided by Douglas's constant criticism. As they pass a turn-off, she glimpses a playing field. Douglas looks back angrily. "You've missed it! It's back there, dummy!"

Pamela tenses and speaks through gritted teeth. "All right,

Douglas, I'm going to turn around so you're on the right side of the road."

The car finally pulls up—opposite the playing field and on the wrong side of the road. Douglas crossly raises his eyes to the heavens, jumps out of the car, and slams the door. He races across the road, forcing an oncoming car to brake and honk. Pamela observes through her side mirror as he narrowly dodges a sticky end.

"It would serve you right, you horrible little shit."

She arrives home to find Stacy and Rupert watching music videos in their pajamas. She tosses the car keys on the kitchen counter and goes to fill the kettle.

Stacy's eyes don't leave the television screen. "There's no bread or milk."

Pamela absorbs this information. Clearly, she's expected to remedy the situation.

Woolworth's on a Saturday morning is not a single girl's domain. In the course of her everyday life, Pamela manages to avoid the big stores, and she normally would never set foot in a mall. Now she has joined the hordes of weekend shoppers who seem intent on playing bumper cars with their carts as they wrestle for the last tin of discounted dolphin-friendly tuna. The queues at the checkouts are so long that they choke the aisles. A professional clown plays a banjo to keep the shoppers distracted. But the banjo doesn't mask the racket of screaming children and price checks, and Pamela's stress levels are peaking. *"It's a good thing I don't have a gun."* That's what my grandmother would have said: *"It's a bloody good thing I don't have a gun."*

Rupert sits up in the cart, with Stacy at the helm. Pamela

trails behind, traumatized. She automatically picks up a liter of low-fat soy milk and tosses it into the cart.

Stacy stares at her choice. "Who's that for?"

"What? . . . Uh . . . Me?"

Stacy scrunches up her nose.

Pamela takes the hint and pulls a liter of whole milk from the shelf. Stacy frowns, dissatisfied. What is she doing wrong? A heavily pregnant woman reaches past her, takes three two-liter containers of milk, and stacks them into her already over-loaded cart. Pamela stares at the cart, which is bursting with multiple, jumbo-size packets of everything. Her eyes widen.

"Big family?"

The woman smiles and nods. "Two boys and a girl."

Pamela's smile fades. She reaches for the hefty milk bottles, then proceeds down the aisles, choosing the largest of every-thing on the shelves. It is unimaginable to her that any house-hold could eat so much, but Stacy doesn't bat an eye.

As they load up a giant box of generic laundry detergent, a twelve-pack of toilet paper, and a packet of jumbo Chux Su-perwipes, Pamela notices that they seem to have mislaid some-thing. "What's happened to Rupert?"

Stacy grimaces. "The usual, probably."

With no idea what Stacy means, Pamela follows her as she steers the cart down the party-goods aisle, passing the soft drinks, potato chips, and corn chips and pulling up at the Twisties display. There, on the floor, in the midst of an ava-lanche of Twistie packets, sits Rupert. He looks up at Pamela and Stacy as they approach, a bright yellow moustache giving his game away.

Stacy pulls him up off the floor and confiscates the open

packet. "What happened to your good-behavior bond? Mum's going to have a fit!" Stacy turns and thrusts the packet at Pamela, who takes a Twistie and pops it in her mouth.

Stacy is shocked.

"You said that bright yellow food coloring is a carcinogenic!"

Pamela shrugs. "Did I? Oh, well, you only live once."

Or is it twice? She doesn't know anymore. She fears that her tentative grip on reality is steadily slipping, like in one of those action movies where the hero is dangling by one arm from a fraying rope over a deadly precipice. In the movies the hero always manages to survive. But right now Pamela identifies not with the hero but with the fraying rope. Wondering when the last strand will snap, she takes another Twistie.

Stacy loads the twelve shopping bags into a cart as the checkout boy processes the last of the shopping. She peers into the last bag. *"Tim-Tams?"*

Pamela tenses. What has she done wrong now? She's sure they don't come in bigger packs than that. "Why? What's wrong with them?"

Stacy shrugs. "I thought we weren't allowed to get them because they cause fights and rot your teeth."

"Well . . . maybe they're just for me."

This is clearly a concept alien to Stacy. Pamela eyes the cigarette shelves with yearning. The checkout boy looks to her. "That's a hundred eighty-two dollars and sixty-five cents."

She just looks at him in shock, then looks in Pamela Dickson's wallet. Twenty dollars and a two-dollar scratch-Lotto ticket—already scratched. She finds a key card and hands it over.

"Check or savings?"

She does a quick eenie-meenie-minie-mo and presses Check.

"PIN number and Okay."

She balks. She has no idea. "PIN number . . . Right . . . PIN number."

She stares at the numbers, her finger hovering.

Stacy goes wide-eyed with embarrassment. "Mum!"

Pamela rummages through her bag. "Maybe I've got a checkbook."

"We don't take checks."

The queue behind them is getting nasty. Stacy is dying. "How could you forget?"

The checkout boy watches Pamela squirm. "It's not your birthday, is it?"

Pamela frowns. What's that got to do with it? "Yes, it was, as a matter of fact—the other day."

The boy nods. "You wouldn't believe how many people use the date of their birthday."

Pamela clicks. She takes a breath and punches in a number. There is a tense pause. Then the processor buzzes into action.

Bit Soon 7
for Alzheimer's

Pamela and Stacy push and pull the overloaded cart through the car park, fighting it every inch of the way, as if it has a mind of its own. Rupert stands up in front, enjoying the tortured ride while licking the inside of the Twisties packet. Pamela struggles to unlock the car.

"What are you doing?" Stacy's standing with her hands on her hips.

Pamela is fed up. "I'm unlocking the car, Stacy. What does it look like?"

"But it's not our car!"

Pamela stands back and regards the car. It looks pretty similar. But she takes Stacy's word for it and moves on to the next dark blue four-wheel-drive. Stacy shakes her head in dismay. "God, Mum, what's with you lately? Menopause?"

As Pamela struggles to open up the back of the correct car,

a sign across the street catches her eye: ANCIENT WISDOM MYSTICS—UNDER NEW MANAGEMENT. She hesitates, then turns to Stacy and tosses her the car keys. "Here, can you load this stuff?"

Stacy's not impressed.

The ethereal chimes on the shop door announce Pamela's entrance. She takes in the hodgepodge of mystical themes: tarot, astrological charts, shaman totems, Egyptian goddesses, crystals, candles, dream-catchers. . . . Even in her hippiest of phases Pamela would have had something cynical to say about the decor. Today she fights her natural skepticism and reminds herself that, given the circumstances, it behooves her to be a little open-minded.

A dowdy middle-aged woman in a pale blue twin-set looks up from her book and smiles. "Hello."

Pamela's heart sinks. She was expecting something just a tiny bit more evocative of the supernatural. This woman looks as if she's just misplaced her bridge partner.

"Hi."

"Lovely day, isn't it?"

"Yes."

The woman correctly intuits Pamela's lack of interest in the weather. "Are you happy browsing?"

Nodding, Pamela picks up a crystal from a bowl of empowering stones and turns it over in her hands, then balks at the price.

The woman watches her. "Is there something I can help you with, dear?"

Pamela returns the crystal to the bowl and smiles uneasily. She looks around nervously. There's another customer browsing through the aura section. She lowers her voice. "Are you . . . do you . . . really know about . . . weird stuff?"

"I'm a spiritual hypnotherapist. I specialize in past-life re-gression." She hands Pamela her card: JUNE DALRYMPLE, DIP SPRT HYP, INTERNATIONAL ASSOCIATION OF MYSTICS. "We also do tarot readings, astrological forecasts, and numerology."

Pamela stares at June's credentials. "I was wondering . . . do you deal . . . with any other sort of life—apart from the past?"

"Well, I have one client who spends quite a lot of his time in the future."

"Really?"

June appears to be utterly earnest. Pamela can't decide whether to get excited or write her off as a loony.

All the while, June smiles sympathetically at her. "What's your problem, dear? Why don't you come and sit down and tell me what it is?"

Pamela looks to this kindly woman, who should be tending a Salvation Army cake stall, and her lips start to tremble. "It's not really a past life. I think . . . it feels . . . it's a present life . . . Another present. I think."

June nods encouragingly. "Another present, you say?"

Pamela doesn't know where to start. She takes a deep breath.

"You see, at one point in my life I had to make a choice. You know: Do I or don't I. . . . And I guess I did. And I didn't. So there are these two paths—or maybe there are thousands. . . ."

She's struck by this thought. What about the Pamela who chose veterinary science instead of journalism? Or the Pamela who chose to take that research job in London? Or the Pamela who wasn't too sick to go on that fatal canyoning trip. . . . She drags herself back to the permutation at hand.

"Anyway, I think I've sort of split into these different worlds."

She checks for a response from June, who's listening intently and gestures for her to continue.

"Basically, it seems there are two of me, I mean, there are probably millions of me, but at the moment I think I'm in the life of another me, you see—the me that ran me over—and I'd quite like to find her—the other me—but I don't know where to start or even—" Frightened, Pamela breaks off.

June prods. "Even . . . ?"

Pamela whispers, "Even if she still exists."

June nods. "I see."

Pamela brightens."You do?"

Solicitously, June takes Pamela's hands in her own, while Pamela's eyes fill with tears. It's such a relief to tell someone, someone who understands.

"I'm sorry, dear, I can see it must be very disturbing for you. But this sort of thing . . . is not really in my field of expertise. Have you tried . . ."

Pamela looks hopefully to her. "Yes?"

". . . a doctor?"

She puts the last of the shopping away and stuffs the plastic bags into their holder. Exhausted and despondent, she fills up the electric jug, switches it on, and starts searching for some herbal tea. Dangling two elderly camomile bags into a mug, she slumps onto a kitchen stool and wonders if June Dalrymple, Dip Sprt Hyp, has hit the nail on the head. Would a trip to a psychiatrist reveal that she is simply having a very elaborate psychotic episode? Is there some kind of medication that would dispel this delusional vision of the house in suburbia and the three children? She suspects not. Maybe she needs shock treatment. One thing is for sure—she definitely needs something stronger than camomile tea.

Just as she takes a sip, Stacy enters and casually grabs an apple from the fruit basket. "Don't you have to pick up Douglas?"

The playing field's deserted. There's no sign of Douglas. Irritated, she gets out of the car to look for him. The kiosk is pulling down its shutters, and the toilet area is closed and locked. She curses. Half a day of motherhood and she's already misplaced a child. At this rate, she should have an empty nest by tomorrow. In fact, she probably shouldn't have left Rupert alone in the car just now. . . .

As she hurries back to the car, Douglas lands with a thud in front of her. His dirty face and the Band-Aid above one eyebrow reflect the aftermath of a brutal game of football. Pamela looks up blankly at the tree from which he has launched himself.

"You're late. I could have been abducted." He stomps past her and gets into the car, slamming the door.

Taking a deep breath, Pamela gets in. "Good game?"

She's met by silence.

"Did you win?"

Douglas looks out the window huffily. "Are we getting something to eat, or what?"

In fluoro-lit fast-food hell, Douglas's mood is restored as he hungrily devours a double bacon cheeseburger, a large order of fries and a thick shake. Rupert is intent on building a high-rise tower with his French fries, while Douglas is in full flight with a commentary of the day's play, chewing as he speaks.

". . . and then she just ran at him—whoomph! He went straight down—face first into the mud. Crunch! You could hear his nose go everywhere. Blood spewing. He had to go to hospital, in an ambulance and everything. You should've seen it. It was so excellent."

Pamela picks at her soggy burger with little enthusiasm. The deafening noise of crying babies, screaming toddlers, and frazzled parents is not an aid to digestion. She can't help but notice that Rupert is jiggling up and down in his seat. She tries to ignore it, but he becomes more and more agitated. She looks to Rupert with dread. He clutches himself. Her suspicions are confirmed.

"I need to go to the toilet."

She considers her options. He's probably a bit young to be allowed into the men's toilets alone. "Douglas, how about you go with your brother to the toilet?"

Douglas laughs, his open mouth full of masticated burger. "No way! That's your job!"

Taking Rupert's sticky little hand, she leads him into the ladies' toilets, hoping he hasn't left his run too late. She stands by as he pulls down his trousers. He turns to her expectantly and she realizes he is too small to reach the toilet bowl. She hoists him up so that he can urinate, but she doesn't position him properly and a stream of urine sprays all over the toilet seat and splashes onto the floor. She grimaces.

The urine trickles to a stop and Pamela jiggles him up and down, then returns him to the ground. She presses the half-flush and turns to Rupert, who stands there with his pants down around his ankles. She pulls them up for him and tucks in his T-shirt. "Okay. Let's go."

Rupert shakes his head. "Not finished."

She is not thrilled by this news. Rupert pulls his pants back down. Pamela wipes the toilet seat dry with a wad of toilet pa-

per, then lifts him onto the seat. "There you go. I'll . . . just be
out here."

She backs out of the cubicle and waits by the basins, staring wearily at herself in the mirror, in utter disbelief. What kind
of atrocities could she possibly have committed in a previous
life to deserve this?

Rupert calls out. "Finished!"

"Well, out you come, then."

There is no movement in the cubicle. She pokes her head
around the door. "Are you finished or not?"

Rupert nods. Pamela has a nasty realization. She braces
herself and enters the cubicle, then pulls reams of toilet paper
from its holder and leans over his bottom with distaste.

"Shouldn't you be able to do this yourself?"

She holds her breath and addresses the odious task with an
unskilled hand.

Rupert runs back to the table and resumes building his
leaning tower of fries. A few minutes later Pamela emerges from
the toilets, having washed her hands thoroughly, twice. She sits
down, quietly proud of a nasty job well done, and is amazed to
discover that she does, indeed, have inner resources when re-
quired.

Douglas slurps the end of his thick shake noisily. "Can I
have another cheeseburger deluxe and strawberry thick shake?"

"If you like."

"What about fries and hot apple pie?"

She shrugs. Douglas is amazed. He grabs her wallet and
races to the counter before she can change her mind.

In the car, Douglas watches as Pamela takes an unexpected
turn-off. "What are you doing? Where are we going?"

"Nowhere. I just need to find . . . somewhere."

She pulls over and tries to get her bearings from the street signs. She pores over the street directory. She was right. They're in the northern suburbs. She plots a course toward the city, daunted by the number of maps she has to turn to, and prays that for once her feeble navigating skills won't let her down. She pulls back into the traffic.

"What? Where are we going? What do you have to find? Mum? *What?* Why aren't we going home?"

"Douglas, do you think you could sit still and be quiet for five minutes?"

There is a moment of silence.

"Why? What are you doing? Mum?! Mum?! Mu-um!"

As they emerge from the harbor tunnel, the streets suddenly become familiar to her and she takes the exit to William Street, up the ramp past the Coca-Cola sign, through the Cross, and turns on to her street, where, as usual, there are no parking spaces. She double-parks outside her block of flats—or, rather, outside what *used* to be her block of flats, but which now closely resembles a building site.

She stares at the gutted building with a cold, creeping sense of alarm. It is fenced off with hurricane fencing and the windows are boarded up. Pamela reads the billboard spanning the frontage: "Available Soon: Six Remodeled City Apartments—One/two bedrooms with en-suite and spa, gourmet kitchen, open living, polished floors, city views, security parking. Ideal for young professionals. Inquiries . . ."

The front entrance is closed and secured with a chain and padlock.

Douglas wiggles in his seat. "What are you doing, Mum? Where are we?"

Chilled, Pamela tries to comprehend what she had been suspecting since the previous evening. She doesn't exist. Pamela Drury's life no longer exists. Not in this world, anyway. This world now consists of endless supermarket queues, French fries, and pooey bottoms.

"Mum? Mum? *Mum?!*"

She turns crankily to Douglas.

"*Yes,* Douglas?"

"Can we go home? . . . I don't feel very well."

Pamela takes note of his greenish hue.

Strangely, she has no trouble finding her way back to suburbia. She drives automatically, numbed by her conclusive discovery that she no longer exists. The children are quiet. Rupert sleeps soundly in the back, and Douglas is ominously silent in the passenger's seat. He's not so bad when he's quiet, Pamela thinks. Maybe she's judged him too harshly. Maybe there's a possibility that she could even grow to tolerate him, with time. It occurs to her that she might have all the time in the world.

Suddenly Douglas rolls down his window, sticks his head out, and vomits with explosive force, narrowly missing a cyclist who swerves in fright. He pulls his head back into the car and wipes his mouth on his sleeve. He looks sheepishly at Pamela. "I think I got some on the car."

Unfortunately, Douglas's spirits improve immediately after being sick, and he proceeds to chatter ceaselessly all the way home. So it is almost with relief, and even a sense of refuge, that Pamela finally turns into the driveway of the Dickson home. Douglas jumps out of the car, slamming the door deafeningly. Pamela can feel a headache coming on.

She wakes Rupert, releases him from his seat, and lifts him

out of the car. She hears the slam of another car door on the street. Rupert wiggles free from her and runs excitedly down the path to the front gate. "Daddy!"

Pamela freezes.

"Hey, Tiger!"

She turns and beholds Robert Dickson, on whom she hasn't laid eyes for thirteen years. He is accordingly older, but he remains easily as handsome. The years have given him . . . substance. Her heart pounds and she feels faint. This can't be for real. She watches Robert drop his luggage, scoop Rupert up into his arms, and sniff his face hungrily, much to Rupert's delight.

"Mmm . . . let me guess. French fries . . . and hot apple pie."

Rupert nods, giggling.

Pamela tries to behave as naturally as possible. She smiles feebly and waves an awkward little wave. "Hi."

Robert looks at her and does a double take. "Wow! Look at you!"

She's unnerved by his gaze—it's as if he's seen through her immediately—and shifts uneasily.

Robert leans over and kisses her on the cheek. "I'm wrecked. Stuck in Melbourne for two hours."

He picks up his case and heads toward the house.

"Did you get the roof fixed?"

She shuts the car door and checks herself in the side mirror. What she encounters is a train wreck. With horror she realizes that she hasn't even had a shower since she . . . arrived. What a great first impression to give a new husband. She drags her fingers through her hair, takes a deep breath, and heads inside.

When in doubt, put the kettle on—that's what her mum always said. Her hand trembles as she holds the kettle under the tap. Robert arrives, goes to the sink, and gets a glass of water.

Pamela makes an attempt at being casual, but her voice cracks a little. "Cup of coffee?"

He shakes his head, downing the glass of water in one go. "I've got to look at some plans before we go out."

"Out?"

"Bit soon for Alzheimer's, isn't it? Your birthday dinner. Remember?"

Pamela nods uncertainly.

"Oh, and I . . . haven't had a chance to get you a present yet. Sorry." He shrugs.

She tries to smile forgivingly. Birthday presents are the last thing on her mind.

In the bedroom, stripped down to her underwear, she searches for something to wear and is disappointed to find that the married mother of three's range is uninspiring. "God! Don't I ever *shop?*"

She tries the underwear drawer, again disappointed at the dearth of black lace. Now, there's an idea for a birthday present if Robert asks her. After all, isn't that what husbands are for?

When he enters the bedroom she jumps, embarrassed by her state of undress.

He takes no notice and heads toward the en-suite bathroom. "What time did you tell Harriet to be here?"

She hasn't the faintest idea of what he is talking about. She looks away uncomfortably as he proceeds to urinate without closing the bathroom door.

Leaving the toilet seat up, he turns on the shower and begins to undress, as Pamela grabs at the pink, fluffy bathrobe that hangs on the back of the bedroom door and pulls it on. She hurries into the kitchen and looks for a Rolodex. She finds a dog-eared address book by the phone, flips to A, and starts working her way through the loose and coffee-stained pages.

Stacy enters with her Walkman plugged into her ears. She observes her mother for a moment. "*What are you doing?*" Stacy switches off her Walkman.

Pamela jumps guiltily. "Uh . . . I'm looking for . . . Harriet's number."

Stacy groans and rolls her eyes. "Do you have to?"

Pamela doesn't need to act innocent. "What do you mean?"

"It's so degrading. Kylie's allowed to mind her little sister. Plus she gets paid!"

Pamela absorbs this with interest. Stacy throws her apple core into the bin across the room. Bull's-eye.

"Mum?"

Pamela is still not used to this form of address. "Hmm . . . ?"

"What's your position on anal intercourse?"

Pamela takes a long look at herself in the wardrobe mirror. She scrutinizes the lines around her eyes, then pats her chin for flabbiness. Does he still find her attractive? It's been thirteen and a half years, after all. Then, again, he has been there all the way from fab to flab, and he probably hasn't even noticed the slow deterioration. Like a frog in hot water, not noticing the rising temperature until it is too late.

She takes a deep breath and closes her eyes. "I am in the rhythm and flow of ever-changing life."

She opens her eyes, unconvinced. Then her heart stops. There, in the mirror's reflection, is her living room. Her old, unrenovated living room. Just as she left it. And she can see herself moving around in it. Only it's not her, because *she's* still standing in Pamela Dickson's bedroom wearing Pamela Dickson's pink, fluffy bathrobe and staring into the mirror. She watches the other Pamela as she approaches the wardrobe and leans toward the mirror to put on bright red lipstick. She has on her old terrycoth bathrobe, and a towel is wrapped around her wet hair. She leans close to the mirror, seemingly oblivious to Pamela. Pamela knocks excitedly on the mirror.

"Hey! Hello! Hey!"

She knocks again.

"Hey! Can you hear me? Hey!"

And suddenly the reflection reverts to Pamela Dickson's bedroom, with the small addition of Stacy, standing at the doorway. "Yes, Mum. I can hear you. What do you want?"

Wide-eyed, Pamela wheels around. "Hmm? . . . Nothing. I mean . . . there was something. But I've forgotten."

Stacy regards Pamela strangely. "You're weird."

Stacy, Douglas, and Rupert are eating pizza in front of *Hey Hey It's Saturday,* while Robert sits reading the newspaper. He glances impatiently at his watch.

Pamela finally enters wearing a close-fitting blue-satin cocktail dress and high heels. Robert looks up from his paper. His eyes widen. "God, does that thing still fit?"

She blushes and kicks herself for not opting for the pantsuit.

Robert folds up the paper.

"Where's Harriet? She's late, isn't she?"

She bites her lip. Stacy pipes up hopefully. "Maybe she's not coming!"

Douglas whoops, "Yes!"

Robert turns to Pamela, appalled. "Don't tell me we don't have a sitter?"

"Well . . . Stacy seems—Stacy is pretty mature for her age. Maybe it's time we gave her more responsibility?"

Stacy's face lights up with shock and amazement, while Robert looks at Pamela as if she's gone mad. But she coolly stands her ground. "That's what I think, anyway."

Robert's about to respond when the front door slams and a plump eighteen-year-old girl rushes in. "I'm so sorry. Go. Hurry. Don't worry about the kids."

Robert is confused, and Pamela wants the ground to swallow her. Harriet dumps her things on the kitchen counter.

"Hi, kids!"

Rupert runs to Harriet and jumps up and down like a puppy around her legs. Douglas ignores her and Stacy shoots Pamela a look that could kill.

A Fly Went By 8

Robert rings the doorbell of an old-style terrace house, as Pamela hovers apprehensively behind him. She'd been hoping for a romantic, candlelit dinner in an intimate French/Japanese restaurant, where they could become re-acquainted over a bottle of champagne, just the two of them. But it isn't looking good. Footsteps echo down the wooden hallway and the door swings open.

"Hey! We were getting worried!"

Robert hands over a bottle of wine and kisses the owner of the footsteps on the cheek. "Sorry, Terri. Baby-sitter."

He casually goes through into the house, while Pamela and Terri stand at the doorway staring at each other. At last, someone familiar! Someone she can talk to. Someone who'll understand. Pamela breaks into a broad grin. It's all she can do not to throw herself into Terri's arms and cover her with kisses.

Terri grins back. "I don't believe it!"

Pamela laughs. "What don't you believe?"

"Your hair! When did you do it? Looks fantastic! Less . . . housewifey."

Pamela touches her hand to her hair, her high spirits taking a dip.

Terri excitedly pulls her inside and leads her to the kitchen. "The food's nothing fancy, you know. I hope you weren't expecting . . ."

Pamela embarrassedly dismisses her attire. "Oh, this? I just felt like wearing it one more time before throwing it out."

"Brings back memories, hey?"

Terri winks conspiratorially. Pamela smiles. She has no idea what Terri is referring to. Perhaps she conceived Stacy in this dress, or spent a night in jail in it, or got horribly drunk and tore it off and ran into the sea on a hot New Year's Eve. . . . Well, she'll never know, but she hopes it's something juicy.

Pamela watches Terri preparing a plate of spring rolls, looking exactly the same as the Terri she knows and loves. Same cheery air, same freckles, same extra pounds. The same Terri with whom Pamela went power-walking just a few days before, when life was normal and Pamela was simply depressed, as opposed to being possessed by the devil.

"So . . . how's Otto?"

Terri smiles lovingly. "He's sleeping. Come and look."

Terri gestures for Pamela to be quiet while she gently opens the bedroom door. Pamela peers in and frowns.

"That's Otto?"

"I know, I know. But you spend a day in hospital and get your balls chopped off and see how you feel. Poor darling. I feel terrible. But he was an animal, chasing after every girl in the neighborhood."

Pamela stares at a huge tabby cat fast asleep in a wicker basket on the floor of the laundry room. She is dismayed by the realization that Otto doesn't exist—at least, not in the human form. Resignedly, she tells herself she might have known nothing in this world could possible be as she knows it. She glances at Terri, who is gazing with adoration at the feline incarnation of Otto. If she doesn't have a baby, has she got a husband? How much more doesn't Pamela know about her best friend?

She nervously follows Terri into the living room, where a party of casually dressed suburban couples is drinking and chatting and eating finger food.

It's like a Christian Fellowship gathering a boyfriend once dragged her to. He wasn't a boyfriend for long, she recalled. Several boisterous toddlers are running wild and emitting the high-pitched squeals that seem to follow Pamela wherever she goes.

She stands out like a sore thumb in her cocktail dress and has the sudden urge to bolt. She looks for the nearest exit.

"Hey! Enter the birthday girl. And whooh! Look at her! Many happy returns, darling!"

Pamela is engulfed in a hug and a very wet kiss. She pulls free and stares at her balding and overweight assailant with a mixture of surprise and horror. It's Big Bad Geoff. "Geoffrey Ballodero!"

He holds his hands in the air in mock self-defense. "Come on, Pammy, isn't a fella allowed a little kiss once a year, or are you gonna have me up on date rape?" He guffaws and slaps her on the backside.

113

A blond woman intercedes. "Hey, you two, do you think we could have a cease-fire for tonight? Happy birthday, Pam. You look terrific."

Pamela smiles weakly. "Thanks . . . Ja——— . . . Janine."

She's astounded to recognize Janine Litski. Miss Blond Early Childhood. As gorgeous as ever. She is further surprised to see Janine wrap an arm around Geoff and give him a loving squeeze.

"Oh, Pam, remind me to get your sitter's number. We're having terrible trouble with Lap. I'm beginning to think she doesn't understand English at all. Is Harriet good with little ones?"

"Who? . . . Oh. I don't . . . I mean . . . Mmm . . . I think so."

Janine seems puzzled by Pamela's unsteady response, but Pamela is now saved by what looks to be a ten-month pregnant woman, who greets her with an affectionate kiss. "Hey, stranger!"

Pamela looks blankly at the woman. "Hey . . . stranger. How are you?"

The woman pats her basketball of a stomach and grimaces. Pamela pretends to empathize.

"Did you remember to bring those things?"

"Uh . . . ?"

"No hurry. Got a feeling this one isn't bursting to come out. Like Rupert. He was late, wasn't he?"

Pamela feels her cheeks reddening. "Mmm."

"How late?"

"Oh . . . uh . . . pretty late."

She's definitely not going to be let off the hook.

"What did you do to give him a move along?"

114

Pamela desperately scans the room for Robert, hoping he is not within earshot when she's discovered as a fraud. She spots him across the other side of the room, drinking beer with Geoff and laughing uproariously.

"What? Oh . . . uh . . . I don't know . . . I drank gin. In the bath. Hot bath. And gin. That normally does it, doesn't it?"

The woman frowns. "I thought that was for an abortion."

A man in a yellow checked shirt with a ruddy complexion joins them. "Hi Pam, how are you?"

Again, she draws a blank. "Hi!"

"You look well. Love your hair like that."

She nods. "Do I? Thank you. So do you . . . Look well."

The man shakes his head wistfully. "I was saying to Judy on the way here, it's been ages since we all got together like this."

Pamela nods, grateful for a name. "Yes, I was thinking the same thing. Haven't seen you and Judy for . . . ages."

"Your place. You and Rob had just got that thingamajig. God, what do you call it?"

"That's right!"

"Been using it much?"

Try as she might, she can't imagine what they are talking about. She nods shakily. "Uh . . . a bit . . ."

An attractive young man in his mid-twenties, wearing ripped jeans and T-shirt, proffers a bottle of wine. "Hello."

Delighted by the interruption, Pamela holds out her glass, which she's drained dry from nerves. "Hello! How are you?"

The young man grins. "Great!"

"You look well."

Terri joins them. "Oh sorry, you two haven't met. Pam, Daniel. Daniel, Pam."

Pamela smiles weakly. "Pleased to meet you."

Daniel and Terri move off together. Judy and Pamela stare after them.

Judy shakes her head in admiration. "Where does she get them?"

Pamela's eyes widen as she watches Terri squeeze Daniel's backside and give him a kiss. "What happened to Leonard?"

Judy raises her eyes to the ceiling. "Which one was he?"

Pamela watches Terri laughing and smiling—and looking disgustingly happy.

Janine pops up again, armed with a plate of salmon and cream-cheese bruschetta. Working on the theory that she won't be able to eat and talk at the same time, Pamela takes a handful.

"So, Pam, what's your news?"

"My . . . news?"

She takes a big bite of bruschetta. Janine watches as a blob of cream cheese sticks in the corner of her mouth and hands her a napkin. "Yes! Feels like we've got out of touch lately. I guess you've had a lot going on."

Pamela nods, mumbling through the bruschetta. "Yes, I have. Lots."

Janine and Judy wait for some details. Pamela racks her brain and reluctantly swallows her mouthful. "Well, what with the kids and everything . . . You know how it is. Will you excuse me? I'm desperate for a leak."

She flees, salmon bruschetta in hand.

Stealing a bottle of champagne out of the ice-filled garbage bin in the kitchen, she finds an upstairs bathroom and locks the door behind her, breathing a sigh of relief as she kicks off her high heels and unzips the too-tight cocktail dress. Settling on the floor against the bathtub, she dines on the remaining salmon and washes it down with champagne, wishing she had a cigarette for after. Her sense of panic subsides proportionally with the level of the champagne bottle as she listens to the hum of the party downstairs and wonders how long it will be before she is missed. It doesn't help, she supposes, that she is the guest of honor and is wearing a look-at-me-I'm-an-alien cocktail dress.

She's polished off the champagne and is resting in the empty bathtub when there's an urgent rapping on the door and the handle rattles. Hastily stumbling out of the bathtub, she struggles with the zipper on her dress and jams it. "Shit!"

The rapping continues. "Hello? Someone in there?"

She gives the toilet a flush for effect. "Just a moment!"

Checking herself in the mirror, she realizes she is more than a little drunk. She struggles with the door and then re-members to unlock it. A woman and a very agitated child with crossed legs wait on the landing. The woman watches Pamela with brows raised as she exits the bathroom, high heels in one hand, bottle of champagne in the other, and dress half un-zipped.

"Pamela! Sorry to rush you. There's a queue downstairs. I'm afraid we couldn't wait."

Pamela smiles. "It's all yours."

The child runs into the bathroom. Her mother follows and closes the door, sneaking a worried glance in Pamela's direc-tion.

Pamela hovers on the landing, loath to descend the stairs. Instead, she wanders into Terri's bedroom. It's strange to see not even a trace of Leonard in Terri's life. No Izis photographs, no

117

Japanese antique furniture, no erotic bedside lamps. She wonders who he's making happy in this life. Not that Terri seems to be suffering from his absence. She looks as infuriatingly happy as ever.

Pamela picks up a familiar framed photo from the dressing table and smiles. It's a picture of her and Terri, aged seventeen, posing proudly on the beach in their up-to-the-minute crocheted bikinis. It was the first day of summer, and the newspaper photographer was roaming the local beaches looking for front page talent. She remembers how ecstatic Terri was to be chosen, having just come off a juice-only diet that lost her eight pounds. She soon put it all back on again and then some, but she always kept the photo framed, as evidence, on her dressing table.

Pamela realizes that it's got to be thirty years since she and Terri met in the kindergarten sandbox, and they've been through thick and thin together ever since, literally. At least in two lives that she can count, and Pamela wouldn't mind betting that Terri is with her in all the others, too.

"There you are! Everybody's been asking where you've got to." Terri stands in the doorway with a drink in her hand.

Pamela puts the photo down. "Sorry. I just came up here. I wasn't feeling very well."

"Oh, my God, the last time I heard you say that, you turned out to be pregnant!"

Pamela smiles. "No chance of that, I'm afraid."

"Good. You've got enough on your hands with the ones you've already got."

Terri turns Pamela around and zips up her dress for her. "Have you got the strength to blow out some candles? I've made your favorite cake."

"Double-chocolate-mousse cake?"

"Do you have another favorite?"

Pamela smiles. At least some things stay the same.

Driving home, she glances at Robert, bursting with questions she knows she can't ask without causing suspicion. His attention is fixed firmly on the road. She gazes at him, lost in the pieces of an unfamiliar jigsaw puzzle. Finally, she bursts. "I can't believe you're still friends with Geoffrey Ballodero!"

Robert groans. "Shouldn't I be? Just because he can get a bit obnoxious . . ."

She grimaces. "He's *exactly* the same. I thought people were supposed to improve with age!"

"I think that's wine. Let's face it, Pam, you've never got a good word for Geoff."

She nods approvingly, relieved to hear that she hasn't succumbed to Geoffrey's slimy charms over the years. "How long have you two been in business together?"

"What? God, I guess it's coming up to twelve years. Not that you've said a civil word to him in all that time."

"I guess we didn't—*don't*—see eye to eye."

Robert snorts. "That's the understatement of the year."

Pamela studies him as he drives. Unlike Geoffrey Ballodero, the years have been kind to Robert. He maintains a full head of hair, graying a little at the sides, which lends an air of maturity that becomes him. His youthful, lanky frame has settled with middle age, and while he's heavier, it's not so much misplaced flab as a general solidness. That's what it is, she thinks—he's more solid, more like a man. Her man.

"Rob?"

"Mmm?"

"Do you ever wonder what would've happened if we hadn't got married?"

"No."

She perseveres. "Well, where do you think you'd be now if I'd said no?"

He shrugs. "Who knows."

She can't resist. "Maybe you would've ended up marrying Janine Litski."

"Give me a break! Janine? Geoff-and-Janine Janine?" He snorts and shakes his head.

Pamela notes with interest that he seems to be genuinely bemused by the idea. He brakes for a red light. Pamela watches him, fascinated. He catches her looking.

She smiles. "Let's do something!"

"Hmm?"

"Let's go dancing!"

"*Dancing?* Are you kidding?"

Pamela can see that dancing has long since been struck off the agenda. "Or what about that place we used to go?"

"What place?"

"Remember? That place with the view—on the way back to your place in Dempster Street. We'd sit in the car and talk all night."

Robert pauses, frowning. "God, what century are you in?"

She realizes her mistake. "Or we could just stop by the harbor and go for a walk and a talk."

He glances suspiciously at her. "Why? What do you want to talk about?"

"Nothing! I just thought it'd be nice to catch up."

"To what?"

"Talk!"

"At ten dollars an hour? It's cheaper to talk at home."

Pamela can't see the logic of this last remark . . .

Until, back home, Robert counts out thirty dollars into Harriet's hand.

"Great! thanks. See you. 'Bye, Mrs. D.!"

Pamela responds, after a pause. "Oh, good-night Hilary—Harriet!"

Robert closes the door and turns out the porch light while Pamela lingers in the hall. He reaches out to turn off the lamp behind her, but he pauses. She smiles nervously, flushed with anticipation and the aftereffects of champagne. She leans to him and tentatively kisses his lips. After pausing, she goes back for more. The taste of his lips is achingly familiar, even across the span of thirteen and a half years. Robert breaks the clinch. Pamela is emotionally dazed.

"It's your hair, isn't it?"

She touches her hand self-conciously to her hair.

He nods. "That's what it is. Makes you look—I don't know—different. Younger or something."

She smiles weakly.

By the basin in the bathroom stand two glasses, one with a red Reach toothbrush in it, and the other with five different brushes in different states of worn-outness. She knows without hesitation that the latter is her glass and wonders what can be said about a person who can't throw out old toothbrushes in case they might come in handy one day. Clearly, Robert had sensibly opted for his own, uncluttered glass. She rinses, spits, and returns the toothbrush to the fold, cupping her hand in front of her mouth and checking her breath. Satisfied, she slides open the bathroom cabinet and scans its contents.

"Come on, Pamela," she mutters. "Haven't you ever heard of safe sex?"

As she searches the shelves, she knocks some Band-Aids and cotton buds into the sink, along with a packet of the contraceptive pill. Picking it up, she sees that the pills have been taken up until the previous day. She actually doesn't want to have Robert's baby, not just yet. At least, not until they've discussed it; it would be their fourth, after all. . . . If she took the next pill, would she be covered? Probably not, she concludes.

She searches the rest of the cabinet. At the back of the top shelf she comes across a flat, round plastic container and a tube of spermicide. She opens it and stares with dread at the white-rubber dome.

After squirting a dollop of spermicidal jelly onto the diaphragm, she smears the gooey stuff around its surface. *How is anybody supposed to feel desirous after messing with this stuff?* The smell of rubber and sperm-killer alone is enough to put one off. Maybe that's the secret of it—contraceptive powers. Tonight, however, nothing can deter Pamela from winding up in the arms of Robert Dickson. Finally.

Bending over, legs apart, blue-satin cocktail dress hitched up around her waist, her face strains as she holds her breath in intense concentration. The diaphragm doesn't seem to want to be inserted. Then, suddenly, it's in. She straightens up gingerly and takes a few steps around the bathroom. Then she does a couple of deep knee bends. Her face contorts. Something isn't quite right.

Down on the bathroom floor, knees apart and feet up against the bathtub, she attempts to re-insert the diaphragm, and she's having trouble visualizing how on earth it is supposed to get to where it has to, and then sproing magically into place. Wouldn't you have more luck tossing Ping-Pong balls into milk bottles? With that thought, the diaphragm slips from her fingers and flies into the air, landing with a splash in the toilet bowl.

"Give the girl a prize."

She lays her head back on the tiled floor, defeated.

A giant T-shirt hangs on the hook on the back of the bathroom door. Going by the giant-koala-with-baby-koala motif and the accompanying slogan, "World's Best Mum," she guesses it's her nightie. Must drive Robert wild with lust, she muses as she pulls it over her head.

Heart pounding, she ventures into the bedroom. True, she's not protected, but last time she looked, Robert didn't seem to be crawling with sexually transmitted diseases. Isn't that why married couples always look so smug? Unlike the chronically single, they're exempt from such worries. As for pregnancy, is it even possible to conceive across universes, or alternate worlds, or whatever warp it is that she's trapped in?

Her stream of deliberation dries up when she finds the lights out and Robert already in bed. Asleep. She pulls back the sheets and crawls in beside him. He stirs and she's on the alert, waiting for him to awake. But no, he sleeps on. She gazes at him in wonder and tentatively moves her hand to his face, almost tracing his lips. He scrunches up his nose in his sleep and readjusts his position. Leaning over him, she breathes in his smell and touches her lips to his. She's startled by a guttural snort and pulls back.

Conceding there will not be any action forthcoming, Pamela lies back on her pillow, disappointed. She closes her eyes, then opens them again. Robert's snoring is unbearable.

The next morning she awakens with her head buried under her pillow. When she opens her eyes, it takes a moment to register where she is. Today, however, the realization doesn't fill her with horror. On the contrary, when she hears Robert's noisy breathing, she's filled with an overwhelming sense of well-being. Emerging from under her pillow, she gently snuggles closer to him. But something gets in her way. She peeps under the sheet and her eyes widen at the sight of Robert's morning erection. Oblivious, he snores on. Pamela wiggles closer, hoping he'll awaken soon.

Then the alarm goes off and he rolls over automatically and slams it quiet. He lies back with his eyes closed. She lies next to him, willing him to roll over and make passionate love to her.

But when he opens his eyes, he springs out of bed, goes to the toilet, pulls on a pair of shorts, grabs his jogging shoes, and leaves the room. She lies back in the empty bed, disappointed. Putting her hand on the warmth he's left, she breathes in his morning smell. Then she notices Rupert standing solemnly at the doorway, watching her. His hair's tousled, like a freshly awakened cherub, and he's clutching Kanga in one hand, a book in the other.

He hesitates for a moment, then approaches the bed and climbs in determinedly next to her, handing her the book and snuggling down. She opens the book and starts reading aloud, hesitating at first.

"I sat by the lake and looked at the sky, and as I looked, a fly went by."

She glances at this angelic little being beside her as she reads. He is utterly engrossed, and, tentatively, she strokes his hair.

Cheek to Cheek 9

Robert pulls the front gate shut and loads the picnic basket into the back of the car, along with Brandy, who starts slobbering excitedly all over the back window. He climbs into the driver's seat, wipes his sunglasses, and adjusts the rearview mirror. Pamela briskly pulls on her seat belt, trying to appear efficient and motherly, while the children are wreaking havoc in the backseat.

"Douglas, get out of the car!" Stacy screws up her nose and frantically winds down the window. Douglas chuckles evilly. Stacy thumps him. "Douglas, you are disgusting! Mum!"

Totally unequipped for settling squabbles, Pamela reluctantly turns to the backseat, but before she can think of anything sensible to say, the pungent smell hits her. "Oh, phew!"

Douglas guffaws. Stacy leans toward Douglas with vehemence. "*Douglas!* You want to die?"

Douglas presses his face toward hers and mimics her. "Stacy! You want to die?"

"Mum! *Mum!*"

Robert glances across impatiently to Pamela. She realizes she is expected to handle the situation, so she turns brusquely to Douglas and clears her throat. "Douglas, do you think you could not do that, please? It's really offensive."

"It wasn't me, it was Brandy."

Robert looks into the rearview mirror and raises his voice forcefully. "Douglas Dickson, stop farting, or you'll be spending the day with your grandmother."

Douglas giggles. Robert turns sharply and nails him with a look. "*I mean it!*"

The smirk slides off Douglas's face and on to Stacy's, while Pamela, startled by Robert's tone of authority, shrinks into her seat.

A spectacular beachside park is the setting for what might be a very romantic picnic, if it weren't for the presence of the three hungry children and the dog, not to mention the ninety-five other families that have had the same idea. Pamela discovers that mothers at picnics have no fun. She scrapes up the remains of barbecued chicken, chips, and coleslaw, and she wipes her greasy hands on a lemon-scented wet wipe from a packet that is clearly a permanent fixture in the picnic basket, along with a squashed packet of Band-Aids, a bottle of bug spray, a pair of tweezers, and an old cotton diaper with some rather nasty stains on it. She pushes the dirty plates toward Brandy, who is lying on the picnic blanket and watching her every move while salivating profusely.

"Go on. Don't tell anyone."

Brandy wags his tail and sets to cleaning the plates. Pamela wonders if this, finally, is a turning point in their relationship.

Rupert has wandered off to a nearby gum tree and is intently feeding Kanga gum leaves and stuffing a handful into her pouch "for later on." Robert, Stacy, and Douglas are playing a raucous game of football. Pamela watches Robert's youthful exuberance as he runs and jumps and shouts exaggerated football jargon at the kids. She envies his ease with the children and reminds herself that she hasn't had quite as much practice.

She jumps up and joins them. "How about a game?"

Play proceeds despite her presence.

She tries again. "Come on! How about it? Girls against guys."

Stacy looks at her as if she's mad. "But you hate football."

"No, I don't. I used to go out with a professional footballer."

Robert looks at Pamela. This is news to him.

She realizes her blunder and starts to backpedal. "Ages ago. High school."

Douglas grunts in contempt. "Huh! You don't even know how to kick the ball. Here, Dad!"

He goes to kick the ball to his father, but Pamela is incensed. Robert looks at her and hesitates. "Why don't you give Mum a go, Douglas? We'll have a proper game later."

Grudgingly, Douglas kicks the ball to Pamela, forcing her to run into a grove of bushes to retrieve it. She picks up the ball, suddenly not so sure of herself. After all, it has been a few years since Brian Paretsky taught her all he knew, and not all the teaching happened on the football field. Concentrating hard, she takes a deep breath and kicks for all she's worth. The contact's good; the ball soars into the air.

Douglas starts running backward to track the ball, but he

trips and falls down heavily on his backside. The ball bounces way beyond him. He gets up, rubbing his posterior in shock.

Stacy punches the air and whoops. "Way to go, Pam!"

Robert looks at Pamela in surprise. She grins and blesses Brian Paretsky.

Light is failing, a hot pink sunset is taking over the sky, and Pamela's now in full swing. She catches the ball and runs for her life toward the goal, with Robert in hot pursuit. Stacy and Douglas run behind, yelling and shouting excitedly.

"Go, Mum!"

"Get her, Dad!"

In a spectacular tackle, Robert brings Pamela down and they wrestle on the ground for the ball. In an instant their eyes lock in complicity. She falls into the moment, breathless, certain in the knowledge that he is in it with her. The kiss is inevitable.

That is, it would have been if Stacy and Douglas hadn't chosen that moment to jump on them.

Romance is rudely scratched from the agenda and bedlam takes over, resulting in a writhing mass of wrestling bodies, screaming, and shouting. Pamela clings stubbornly to the ball. Rupert joins the melée and Brandy races around them, barking excitedly. The family ends up sprawled out on the ground, exhaustedly puffing and panting under the dark pink sky. Pamela feels inexplicably happy.

It is dark and cool when they finally fold up the picnic blanket and make for the road home. The mood inside the car has changed considerably since the outgoing trip. Douglas and Rupert have fallen fast asleep, and Stacy stares pensively out the window, trying to battle the Sunday-night blues that inevitably herald the new school week. Even Brandy has crashed out, his nose squashed up against the picnic basket.

Pamela watches the oncoming headlights, a delicious exhaustion enveloping her. She's trying to recall the last time she had such a good time. And can't. Robert looks across to her, reaches out, and rests his hand on her thigh. She covers his hand with hers, squeezes it, and dozes off.

At home she carries Rupert from the car to his bedroom. Still fast asleep and hugging Kanga, his head hits the pillow heavily. She undresses the sleeping boy, covers him, and removes a gum leaf from his hair. Although she doesn't feel quite at ease with Rupert when he's awake and has yet to forgive him for his incompetence in the bathroom, she experiences a wave of maternal stirrings as she gazes at him. She hesitates, then tenderly strokes the delicate perfection of his porcelain cheek.

She's interrupted as Robert enters the room, carrying Douglas across his shoulders. Douglas is kicking and struggling and trying to unbalance Robert by covering his eyes with one hand and tearing his hair out with the other. Robert staggers to the bed and unceremoniously unloads him. Pamela watches as Robert pushes Douglas under the bedclothes and pins him into bed.

Douglas resists energetically. "Get off, Dad! Get off!"

Amid the horseplay, Robert resorts to mock-strangling his oldest son before planting a big sloppy kiss on his head. Douglas wiggles and guffaws with laughter.

Pamela watches from the doorway, frankly fascinated by this new Robert, and impressed by the extra dimensions to the young man she knew all those years ago. The added responsibilities of fatherhood have clearly sobered him, and yet there's a wonderful childlike energy he seems to have absorbed from the

129

children. It's not quite how she had imagined him all these years. How could she? But one thing is for sure—she still finds him devastatingly attractive.

She stands up from a deep knee bend, snapping shut the plastic diaphragm container. Triumphant.

Climbing into bed, she keenly observes Robert as he strips down to his boxer shorts and T-shirt. Aching with anticipation, she can barely lie still, like a child waiting to open a Christmas stocking. Unaware of her eager gaze, Robert climbs into bed. Pamela looks away demurely, waiting for the inevitable. She tingles as she remembers their unmistakable connection earlier in the park. If only the children hadn't been there, fireworks would surely have erupted. Just like the first time she and Robert made love. She'd been hanging out for it then, too. In the end, she hadn't been able to wait any longer and had propositioned Robert boldly in the front seat of his old Ford Falcon. Actually, now that she thinks back on it, there weren't really any fireworks. In fact, she can't remember much about the first time at all, except that she let Robert use a condom because she was too embarrassed to admit she'd gone on the pill in anticipation.

But Pamela knows that this first time is going to be different. They are going to do it in their marriage bed, for starters, and they're both bringing years more experience to the exercise. She tries to control her excitement as she sneaks a glance at Robert. He plumps up his pillow, then reaches for his reading glasses and a bulging manila folder. She watches as he settles down to read. Frustration and disappointment clutch at her stomach as she starts to suspect that he's not even going to say good-night to her, let alone make a sexual advance. What's the story? Does he feel nothing for her? Was she imagining the energy that flashed between them in the park?

"What's that?"

Robert glances briefly at her. "What? . . . Oh, the feasibility reports for the Bouvier job. Someone's got to have been paid to come up with some of these findings. Bloody ridiculous!"

She watches him for a moment, trying to muster some composure. "Will you be long?"

Robert sighs. "I thought the light didn't bother you? I've got a meeting first thing."

"Oh, no, it doesn't. It's just . . ."

Robert turns a page, then scribbles a note in the margin. Pamela can see she's lost his attention and decides to wait it out. There's no way she's going to be able to sleep in the state she's in, and anyway, how long can it take to read a report? "Actually, I feel like reading myself."

She picks up the paperback lying on her bedside table, wipes the dust off the cover, and squints at the title: *Men Are from Mars, Women Are from Venus.* It's a title that she has intentionally not read. She can't stand those horrid self-help books that presuppose the existence of a committed relationship. She hasn't had one of those recently and really didn't need to be reminded. As far as she was concerned, the good men never left Mars. But all that's changed now, and she's got one, even though she did indeed have to change universes to find him.

Pamela turns to Pamela Dickson's bookmark with smug interest. After a moment she turns back to the beginning and starts at page one.

An hour later Robert closes his file, yawns, and takes off his glasses and puts them away. He looks across to Pamela, who is

131

fast asleep over her book. He leans over and gently pulls the book away.

She awakens with a jolt. "What?"

"You were asleep."

"No, I wasn't!"

Pamela turns over and, to his surprise, snuggles up to Robert. She hesitates, then kisses him, tentatively at first, then with increasing vigor. He's taken aback by her ardor. She pulls her koala nightie off, then proceeds to remove his T-shirt. Then she kisses his chest, his stomach, and keeps moving steadily south. She divests him of his boxer shorts, then goes to work under the sheets. Robert is clearly unused to such attentions and his eyes widen with wonder and delight. Curious, his eyes go to the book she has been reading. . . .

The book falls to the floor as they make love with hip-grinding enthusiasm. Robert's desire has well and truly been kickstarted. Pamela moves with him, totally overwhelmed by desire and emotion. She's filled with the sense that she's come home. He smells and feels so familiar, apart from his slightly thickened waistline and new love handles. While he kisses her face, her ear, her neck, she moans and arches and catches sight of the wardrobe mirror. Is it her imagination, or did she catch a fleeting glimpse into her old apartment?

With a thud, she falls out of the moment, her attention split between Robert and the mirror. But as she strains for another look, all she can see in the reflection is herself and Robert making love. She watches him kissing her ardently and wonders why she feels like a child who has cheated at Monopoly and won.

Disturbed, she turns away from the mirror and makes an effort to reenter the lovemaking. Robert is blissfully unaware of her brief absence.

Later, she lies entwined with Robert, who is in a state of pleasant stupor. A tear trickles down her cheek and splashes onto his chest.

Robert feels it and frowns. "What's the matter?"

She quickly wipes a tear away, but another one follows close behind. "Nothing. Nothing's the matter. It's just . . ."

Robert is concerned, pulling himself up on his elbow to see her face. "Just what?"

She sniffs. "Just that . . . I've always loved you. Since forever."

Robert is surprised and affected by this declaration and responds with a tender kiss. As they snuggle together, he absently caresses her hand. He pauses. "Where's your ring?"

Pamela freezes. "I lost it."

"*Lost* it?"

She grimaces. "No . . . well . . . I mean . . . it fell off . . . I must've lost weight. So . . . it's at the jeweler, being resized."

He's surprised, but he appears to accept her clumsy explanation. She distracts him with a passionate kiss.

The kitchen is a hive of breakfast activity. Douglas blades across the floor as he hurriedly throws peanut-butter sandwiches together; Stacy's gobbling down toast while buttering the next piece. Robert is eating Muesli, making coffee, and trying to listen to the news.

Douglas hastily wraps his sandwiches in a blanket of plastic wrap and stuffs them into his bag, then blades out of the kitchen. "See you."

Stacy grabs a piece of fruit off the counter and shouts after him, "Thanks for waiting, dickhead!"

Robert sighs and shakes his head.

Meanwhile, in the bathroom, Pamela's nose is upturned as she leans over Rupert and wipes his bottom.

"Tell me, at exactly what point do you learn how to do this yourself?"

At the front gate, Pamela sees Robert and Rupert off. She cuts quite a Doris Day, having found in the wardrobe a pair of fluffy pink bunny slippers to go with her fluffy pink bathrobe. She smiles. The spring flowers are blooming, the birds are singing, the sky is blue, and all is well in the world of suburbia.

Robert kisses her on the cheek. "See you."

To his astonishment, she pulls him back and kisses him long and passionately on the mouth. She releases him and gives a little wave. "'Bye, dear. Have a nice day."

Robert nods dumbly.

"'Bye, Rupert!" Rupert turns and gives her a faintly disapproving look.

She watches as they walk down the footpath toward the preschool and train station, then ambles back to the house, past the climbing roses and hyacinths, breathing in their giddy perfume and grinning from ear to ear.

Pamela spreads her toast with chocolate spread on one half and colored sprinkles on the other, feeling deliciously depraved. Cup of coffee in one hand, toast in the other, she roams around the house, cheerfully snooping and soaking up her new milieu. She stops at the large gold-framed wedding photograph and scrutinizes the image of herself as a glowing bride. She carefully replicates the brilliant smile. Brandy dozes in a patch of sunlight, one eye on Pamela. Pamela turns, aware she is under surveillance. He throws her a knowing look.

She washes the dishes to the sound of talkback radio—a

heated discussion about working mothers—and finds herself taking an unprecedented interest in the topic. She contemplates ringing in and having her say, but she realizes that perhaps she's come to motherhood a little late to have a fully informed opinion. She pulls the plug, wipes the countertop, and appraises the sparkling kitchen with satisfaction, then switches radio channels, finds a very golden oldie, and swoons, turning up the volume.

"Heaven, I'm in heaven, and my heart beats so that I can hardly speak . . ."

She waltzes dreamily through the kitchen as she dries the dishes. "Da-de-dum-de-da-de-happiness I seek . . . when we're out together dancing cheek to cheek . . ."

She drops the dirty tea towels into the empty washing machine, closes the lid, and washes her hands in the laundry sink. Enough housework for one morning, she concludes, before laying eyes on the soaring mountain of dirty clothes lurking behind the laundry door. Reluctantly, she supposes that clearing the mountain is a duty that a stay-at-home mother should properly do. It does cross her mind to look up the nearest laundromat in the Yellow Pages, but she suspects the housekeeping money doesn't run to that.

To the sound of *South Pacific*'s "I'm gonna wash that man right outa my hair," she sorts the dirty clothes until she has a dappled mountain range of whites, darks, and coloreds, sheets and towels. She agonizes over a black-and-white-striped T-shirt before giving it a pile of its own. Then she bundles up the things that need hand-washing and returns them to the bottom of the wash basket. She surveys the piles of wash with dissatisfaction. Some of them won't make full loads.

Wading through the alien landscape of the boys' bedroom,

she searches for grubby castoffs. Not having grown up with brothers, she finds the boyish junk alien and marvels at the evidence of stereotypical pursuits, most notably the violent array of sabers and guns, homemade and otherwise. How could she have got to the point of allowing such horrors into the house? She appraises a junior pair of track pants for dirt, then brings them to her nose and nearly passes out.

Pushing open the door to Stacy's room, she knows full well that she is forbidden to enter. But wild horses couldn't keep her out . . . while Stacy is at school. She surveys the room and is besieged by nostalgia. A schizophrenic combination of outgrown dolls, dolphin posters, peace signs, and pop idols crowd the room. No poster of Robert Redford graces the walls, but Pamela assumes that the smoldering, dark-haired, twenty-year-old from *Party of Five* is the latter-day equivalent. A fantastic collage covers one whole wall and reaches across the ceiling. An overstuffed bookshelf doubles as home to a menagerie of tiny collectible animals of all descriptions.

Pamela scans the bookshelf and pulls out a dogeared copy of *The Lion, the Witch, and the Wardrobe.* She opens it up and is moved to read the faded, childish handwriting on the first page: "This book is the property of Pamela Drury." Tracing the writing with her finger, she remembers the day Aunt Rose gave her the book and how it ignited her passion for the Narnia chronicles. She remembers, too, the wet afternoons spent sitting in her wardrobe, beseeching the great lion Aslan to allow her entry to the mystical land of Narnia, as Peter, Susan, Edmund, and Lucy had done before her. Or the days when she was sick in bed, and she'd stare and stare at the picture of the sailing ship on the wall, desperate to dissolve into the world of the picture, as Lucy and Edmund and Eustace had done in *The Voyage of the Dawn Treader.* Sadly, her wishes fell on deaf ears and were later assigned to childish fantasy. But now, standing in her other self's daughter's bedroom, such childish beliefs seem remarkably plausible.

Pamela had kept the books with her through the years, with the vague thought that one day she would pass them on to her child. . . . She feels a lump forming in her throat and carefully returns the book to its place.

She exits Stacy's room with a head full of memories and an armload of wash. At the end of the hallway she notices a closed door. Curious, she opens it and peers inside, then drops her bundle of wash at the doorway and enters.

Inside is a small, cluttered study. Crammed bookcases and piles of paperwork are reminiscent of Pamela's own study. But unlike her study, the walls are virtually bare. She recognizes the lone adornment—the framed newspaper clipping of young Pamela as "Cadet of the Year."

She pushes past an ironing board, topped by an overflowing basket of unironed shirts, and approaches the untidy desk, which is partly hidden by a large vinyl dust cover. Lifting the cover, she discovers a computer and printer, and she marvels at the prehistoric technology before her. Pamela can't imagine anyone actually using this dinosaur of a computer. She pulls up a chair and pokes around the desk and drawers inquisitively. What did Pamela Dickson do in this half-baked study—besides the ironing? Has she kept up her writing as a hobby? Does she dabble in creating children's stories? Or is this simply an unused testament to her wasted potential?

From the left-hand drawer she pulls out a pair of purple ear muffs, which she regards curiously, not being a big skier herself, and recalling that Robert had never been very keen on the

137

cold. In fact, the one time she dragged him to the Snowy Mountains he complained all the way, saying snidely that if God had meant them to visit the snow, he wouldn't have made it so expensive. If she remembers correctly, an icy weekend ensued. She tosses the muffs back into the drawer.

To her right she is surprised to find the latest issue of *Now Woman,* the glossy magazine Pamela has long abhorred. Curious, she opens the magazine and flips through it. It falls open at a double-page article with a picture of a gorgeous woman in sexy underwear. She reads the headline: "Love And Marriage— How to Keep the Marriage Alive," by Pamela Dickson.

She drags her eyes from the byline and scans the copy with growing incredulity.

"You've had the whirlwind romance and the fairy-tale wedding. But what's a girl to do when the honeymoon is over? Here are ten surefire ways to keep the magic alive. . . ."

Is it possible that she actually writes this rubbish? That she is *paid* to write it? She flips through a pile of back copies in the Out tray and finds more examples of Pamela Dickson's handiwork.

"Cosmetic Surgery—The Answer to Your Problems?"

"Jealousy—Is the Green-eyed Monster Lurking Under Your Bed?"

"What to Do When You're Keener Than He Is . . ."

Pamela is dumbstruck by the endless stream of moronic, reactionary drivel with her name on it. As she pores over "Do You Make Out with the Lights Off?," she is startled by the strident ring of the old-fashioned telephone on the desk. She hesitates to answer it, but on the tenth ring she succumbs.

"Hello?"

"Pamela—Deirdre." The voice on the end of the phone is brusque.

Pamela is none the wiser. "Hello . . . Deirdre."

"Where are you?"

Pamela thinks for a moment. "I'm . . . at home."

"I've got ten-thirty down here."

"Ten-thirty?"

"Look, can you be here in half an hour?" *Click.*

Pamela puts the phone down uncertainly. Who's Deirdre when she's not barking through a phone line? She focuses on the magazine in front of her and flips to the Contents page, runs her finger along the bottom, and squints at the small print. She stops.

FEATURE EDITOR: DIERDRE REYNOLDS.

Rifling through the wardrobe, she tries to guess at what would pass for a suitable outfit for a meeting with someone she doesn't know at a workplace she's never been to. She strains to remember what Pamela Dickson was wearing when they crashed into each other. Cream trousers and a denim overshirt. She had assumed that was a mum outfit, not a work outfit, but then she didn't know that Pamela had a job, least of all a job for the country's top-selling women's glossy. Maybe that was what had brought Pamela Dickson to the city on the day they collided.

She settles on a beige suit that probably dates back to the early nineties but is fairly nondescript and at least fits well. She looks at herself in the mirror and cringes.

"Here goes nothing."

The Modern Woman 10

The massive revolving doors of the National Consolidated Press building spit Pamela into the immense foyer of a glass skyscraper. She enters with trepidation, taking in the plush surroundings and the glossy framed cover sheets of the high-profile magazines and journals published by the company.

The security guard nods to her and she nods back, making for the lifts. Still within sight of the security guard, she presses Up and casually steps back to wait. Out of the corner of her eye, she frantically scans the directory on the wall: NOW WOMAN—44.

She emerges at the forty-fourth floor into a hectic open-plan office. Nobody shows any sign of recognizing her as she walks through what feels like a minefield of desks and partitions. She makes it to the editor's office, where a smartly dressed middle-aged woman is busy at a large desk.

"Excuse me, I'm—"

The woman looks up. "Thought you'd been hit by a bus or something."

Pamela smiles weakly. "Sorry, I didn't realize—"

"Better late than never."

The woman smiles and returns to her work. Pamela stands there uncertainly. Obviously, she's in trouble, because she missed the ten-thirty meeting. Now she supposes she'll have to wait until Deirdre deigns to talk to her. She didn't even ask her to sit down while she waits. Pamela muses that this is precisely the kind of power game that must go on in these big corporations. She catches herself thinking fondly of *Focal Point,* where at least Max calls a spade a bloody shovel, and doesn't mind using it, for that matter.

Finally, the woman pauses from her work and looks up at Pamela, surprised to see she is still there. "Go right in. She's waiting for you."

Pamela does a three-sixty before seeing a large glass portal behind her.

She pokes her head into the office, which has a panoramic view of the Harbour Bridge and Opera House. She has a flash of déjà vu. This is her fantasy office! A girl in her mid-twenties, private parts barely covered by a bright red miniskirt, is bending over some cover artwork. Surely this can't be the features editor.

"Deirdre?"

The young woman turns and eyeballs her coldly. "Do you want to talk about it?"

"I . . . er . . . don't think so."

"Sit down."

Pamela sits obediently while Deirdre sinks into her huge

black-leather swivel chair, crosses her sheer-stockinged legs, and swivels menacingly.

"Look, Pam, it's not like you to miss a deadline, so if you're having problems . . . ?"

"No, no. I'm just not quite sure . . . maybe if you could give me an idea . . ."

Deirdre is scornful. "What's so hard? 'The Modern Woman.' Let me see: Now that we've bullied the guys into changing the sheets and leaving the toilet seat down, what do we really want?" She looks to Pamela, as if it's obvious.

Pamela waits expectantly.

"Romance! Femininity! . . . blah-blah-blah. You can do it on your head."

Pamela nods and smiles, appalled.

"We need this one fast or we'll miss the issue. Friday. Okay?" She picks up the phone. "Jools, get me Joe Nathan."

Pamela realizes she is dismissed.

As she reaches the door, Deirdre calls out, "Oh, and Pam, make sure you tie it in with next season's look. Barbara will give you the pics."

Pamela backs out of Deirdre's office and returns to the middle-aged woman she now realizes is Deirdre's assistant.

Barbara pulls a manila folder from her In tray and slides it toward Pamela. "How are the kids?"

"Oh, fine, thank you."

"You've got to bring your little one in again. He's priceless. Talk about a chatterbox!"

Pamela smiles. Can she really be describing Rupert? The most he's ever said to her is that he needs to go to the toilet.

Avoiding eye contact with the other passengers lest she is supposed to know any of them, she gets into the lift, occupying herself by looking through the folder of leggy shots that are an excuse for next season's fashions. She shakes her head, wondering how much she gets paid for writing rubbish for this place. Probably double her *Focal Point* wage, at a fraction of the hours. So Pamela Dickson not only married the love of her life, had the children, but got herself a fabulously well paid job with a glossy magazine to boot. Pamela Drury feels the damp of depression rising.

The lift stops at the next floor. All but one person get out, bumping Pamela as they pass, causing her to drop the folder. The photographs spill out all over floor. "Shit!"

She bends down to collect them while a man gets in and greets the remaining passenger. "Mate."

"G'day, mate."

He flips through a magazine and shakes his head. "Christ! Some of the rubbish this place puts out. Listen to this: 'You've had the whirlwind marriage and the fairy-tale wedding. But what's a girl to do when the honeymoon is over?"

Pamela's ears begin to burn as he continues.

"'Here are ten surefire ways to keep the magic alive.' Jesus! Who writes this crap?"

Pamela stands up. "I do."

He curses silently, then turns to her. She meets his eyes, then catches her breath. Ben Monroe. She can't believe her eyes. Ben, on the other hand, shows no signs of knowing Pamela, but he is clearly embarrassed by his gaffe.

The lift stops and his mate gets out, giving Ben a mock congratulatory slap on the back on his way out. The doors slide shut. There is an awkward moment while Pamela absorbs the coincidence and Ben bites his tongue. He shifts uneasily. "Would you believe me if I said I didn't mean—"

"No. You're right. It *is* crap."

He smiles weakly, then turns his attention to the lift's progress. Pamela can't help staring at him. He's in trousers and sports jacket rather than self-defense gear, but he still has the same disheveled appeal.

"So, you're a journalist?"

Ben nods.

"Who do you write for?"

"*Speed Weekly*. Features, mostly."

Pamela's brow furrows. "*Speed?* The sports rag?"

Ben nods, proudly.

Pamela is disappointed. "Well, *that's* hardly investigative journalism."

Ben is obviously taken aback.

At the ground floor Pamela exits the lift. Unfamiliar with the territory, she turns right and is faced with a dead end. She does an about-face and smiles with embarrassment at Ben, who is watching her.

"I always do that."

Ben looks at her quizzically.

"Look, I was just going out for a caffeine hit. Would you like to . . . I mean, if you've got time . . . my treat. It's the least I can do."

She hesitates. He's probably married in this life, too, and she's not going to make a fool of herself a second time. Besides which, she sternly reminds herself, she is currently married to the man she loves. "No, I don't . . . think so."

Ben nods, dismissing the idea. He goes to turn away, then stops and holds out his hand to Pamela. "I'm Ben, anyway. Ben Monroe. I prefer it to 'that arrogant bastard.'"

She nods, knowing full well who he is and what he stands

for. Trouble. Ben awkardly withdraws his hand. But she has a change of heart and puts out her hand. "Pamela. Pamela Dru-Dickson!"

They shake hands, their eyes lock, and Pamela finds herself wondering where the harm is in an innocent cup of coffee.

In a busy cafe looking out on the sparkling harbor, she stirs her cappuccino with exaggerated concentration, her mind reeling with the strangeness of the situation.

Ben watches her stirring and stirring and stirring. "You been writing that . . . stuff for long?"

"Crap, you mean? God, no. To tell you the truth . . ." She realizes she can't. "I've done other stuff. What about you?"

He nods. "Fair while."

"Why sports? Didn't you want to tackle the heavy stuff? You know, expose corruption, right all wrongs!"

Ben looks at her inquiringly and she tries to cover.

"I mean, if you're going to be a journalist, aren't there more important things to write about than this week's groin injury?"

"What? Like cosmetic surgery, how to please your man, and the best way to lose those extra pounds?"

Pamela takes the point. She can't very well defend herself, but she's obviously hit a nerve.

Ben becomes pensive. "Actually, it's funny you should say that, because I did have high ideals when I started out. Didn't you?"

She nods. Trouble is, she never grew out of them.

"Somehow I fell into sports. Actually, I enjoy it. Most of the time. Plus I get a lot of free travel."

Pamela licks her spoon clean of froth and sets it down. "Does your wife mind? . . . You traveling?"

"I suppose she might—if I had one."

He smiles cheekily, while Pamela tries to absorb this information. Just her luck that in this life he's available and she's not. What the hell is fate trying to say to her?

Ben glances at her naked wedding finger. "What about you?"

She shifts her hand and sips her coffee evasively. "Oh, no, I don't get much free travel at all."

Outside the cafe, a Japanese honeymoon couple pose for their wedding photographs against the spectacular harbor backdrop. The heavily made-up bride sparkles in her rented white-satin gown. The groom holds her stiffly, while the photographer tries to push them and prod them into a romantic tableau, as if they are made of pipe cleaners.

Pamela glances at Ben as he watches them, apparently amused. "Have you ever been married?"

"Me? Nope. Came close once. A long time ago. Another life. Sophie. We were students together. I was going to be a school-teacher, believe it or not. Anyway, we were crazy for each other. Nearly did the whole bit—marriage, children, matching pajamas."

"What happened?"

"She was hit by a car. Drunk driver. Just before graduation. Killed instantly." Ben looks away.

Pamela is lost for words. "Oh, my God. I'm sorry. That's awful."

"Yeah, well . . . I went off the deep end. Chucked teachers' college. Traveled the world. Went in another direction." He stares out at the harbor.

Pamela is struck by this version of events. This life has certainly not been kind to Ben, and indeed, it has etched a sadness into him that she had not recognized. She remembers the image of Ben Monroe in her world, with his wife and little children standing at the window, delighting in the thunderstorm. Was that Sophie? How do you ever recover from losing someone who means that much to you? If only Pamela could tell Ben that somewhere in another world his story is playing out happily ever after. But he'd think she was crazy.

Pamela hesitates. "Do you ever wonder what your life would be like if . . ."

"She was still alive? Oh, only every day. I mean, there have been others, but I guess you could say that Sophie was the love of my life."

He looks at Pamela and shakes his head in disbelief.

"Jesus! You're good at this!"

She doesn't know what he's talking about. "Good at what?"

"What are you going to call it? 'Men Who Talk Too Much?'"

She grimaces, dogged by her new "glossy" persona.

They part with a too-formal handshake at the revolving doors of the press building, and Pamela walks back to the car pondering life's ironies. Why has she met Ben in this life, and what does it mean? Nothing, probably. It's a crazy coincidence, and besides, what does it matter? She has Robert now. She's not in the market for a man in this life. It's just a little hard to shake the habit, that's all.

She pushes Ben to the back of her mind and concentrates on a more pressing issue.

Walking right past the *Now Woman* display, the bridal magazines, women's health and pregnancy, and the home-renovating journals, she stops at the cooking section of a large suburban news agency. The choice is daunting, from the *Vogue Wine and Food Cookbook* to *The Women's Weekly Guide to Cooking with Mince*. She flips through *Cooking for Crowds, Recipes My Mother Gave Me*, and *Microwave Cooking at Its Best* and feels completely confused. All she is looking for is something dead easy and fantastically impressive.

It would be a lot simpler to do what she always does when she entertains—that is, find the nearest gourmet take-away, buy something terrific, and pass it off as her own. But that's cheating, and she doesn't feel like cheating anymore. She wants to do it right—like Pamela Dickson does it. Besides, there is something special about a home that is infused with the smell of cooking.

She is reminded of the trick that her mother confessed to one Christmas after one too many whisky sours. The secret of her success. If it got to six o'clock and she hadn't got dinner started, she'd throw some onions on to fry, so that when her beloved—but often tired and cranky—husband stepped through the door, he'd be met by the welcoming aroma of cooking, which never failed to put a smile on his face. "And then you could throw him frankfurters and toast and he wouldn't know the difference."

She settles for the latest issue of *Gourmet Traveller*, chooses a recipe to die for, and goes shopping for a duck.

Rupert has chosen the kitchen floor as the site for his railway, and is in the process of building the tracks around Brandy and through Pamela's legs, which is a bit tricky because the latter have a habit of moving. In the next room Douglas is noisily blasting a Nintendo enemy to kingdom come; Stacy has shut herself in her bedroom, with her ghetto blaster playing at full voltage, and the *Gourmet Traveller* is lying spreadeagle on the counter.

Pamela has tomatoes blanching, onions sautéing, asparagus steaming, and she is having terrible trouble skinning a chicken. It turns out that ducks are not available on short order in outer suburbia. Her stress level rises as she watches the clock and dreads Robert coming home and witnessing the state of the kitchen.

"Toot-toot! Chugga-chugga-chugga-chugga." Rupert stages a spectacular crash between his train and a fully loaded bus. The tiny passengers spill out all over the floor.

Pamela tries to relax as she crunches one of them under-foot. "Rupert, sweetie, why don't you take your train out of the kitchen? Please?"

The telephone rings. She hurriedly wipes her slimy hands, steps over Rupert, and answers with caution. "Hello? . . . *Mum!* Hi! . . . No, no, it's just good to hear your voice. . . . What? . . . Do I? Actually, I'm just in the middle of getting dinner . . ."

She wedges the phone under her chin and pulls the as-paragus off the heat.

"No, no . . . Oh, the kids are . . . fine. Yes, he's fine. Mum, how many cups of rice do you need for five people? . . . Do I? . . . I mean, of course I know, but you always make the exact right amount."

She stirs the burning onions and tries to get back to the chicken peeling. "I don't know . . . Busy. I never realized how— Relax? . . . What do you mean, I take on too much?" She can't believe her ears. "Let me get this straight—you think I should make more time for *myself*? What are you trying to say?"

She stops what she is doing and listens to her mother's critique.

"I think we do share the load. He does help! Well, I'm sure he does more than Dad ever did. . . . What? You never did like Rob, did you? . . . I'm *not* being sensitive! . . . Okay, okay, I know you don't. I know you do. . . . Okay. You, too. 'Bye, Mum."

Incredulous, she puts the phone down. Here she is, happily married with children, and her mother still isn't satisfied. She can't win. Suddenly, a bouquet of red roses appears under her nose. She turns in surprise. Robert grins and kisses her adoringly, pressing her up against the kitchen cupboards until she has no doubt of his physical state. Wow! Pamela thinks. The smell of cooking onions might put a smile on their face, but the smell of burning onions drives them wild!

She nervously presents the dinner, having managed to pull it together from the brink of disaster. It almost resembles the picture in *Gourmet Traveller,* if you travel to the other end of the room and squint your eyes. She's also uncovered the best crockery and has set the table with candles, and flowers from the garden, in a desperate attempt to create a romantic dinner for . . . five.

Robert's eyes widen at the lavish meal. He whistles. "God! What's this?"

Pamela strikes a match and lights the candles in the centerpiece. "Oh, nothing much. Just duck-something-French. Only with chicken. Stuffed. I don't know what it'll be like."

Stacy is curious. "Did *you* cook this?"

Douglas sticks his nose in his meal suspiciously. "Smells funny." He pokes at it and brings a forkful to his mouth. He chews with care, then at long last delivers his verdict: "It's edible."

Pamela looks to Robert. He chews, swallows, and nods appreciatively. "Mmm!"

He is clearly impressed, and she grins proudly.

She never knew that cooking could be so rewarding. Outside it is raining. Inside, Robert is attending to all her bodily desires. Pamela is delighting in having an ongoing sex life with someone she loves, even if the circumstances are a little inexplicable. She has turned the lights out, which is less romantic, but at least it avoids the problem of the reflection in the wardrobe mirror. Unfortunately, she is acutely aware of the presence of the children in the house and notices that Robert makes virtually no noise, which she finds a little disconcerting. She wonders how indeed married people keep the magic alive when there are three innocent (or almost) children sleeping down the hallway, and she reminds herself to read what Pamela Dickson has to say about it in *Now Woman*.

Just as she pulls the duvet over both of them to muffle her moans, the telephone rings with all the grace of an air-raid siren. Robert groans, annoyed, but makes no move to answer it. The phone keeps ringing. Pamela isn't sure of the protocol. She stops what she is doing. It's not going to go away.

"Should we get that?"

Robert grunts and rolls over in irritation.

She wiggles from under the bedding, turns on the lamp, and reaches for the phone. "Hello?"

She freezes at the sound of Ben's voice. She turns away from Robert, wondering how he got her number. "Hello. . . . No, no . . . Well, it's just . . . I'm right in the middle of . . . work, and I've . . . er . . ."

She is distracted by Robert as he continues to nibble her toes.

"Um . . . got a deadline that I'm really pushing to make, so . . ." She pulls her foot away.

"No, no, that's okay. . . . Yep, sure. 'Bye."

She hangs up, face flushed.

Robert lifts his head from under the covers. "Who was that?"

Pamela's mind races. "Terri!"

Robert frowns. "At this hour? Why didn't you just tell her we were bonking?"

Pamela is flustered. She rolls back toward Robert. He hesitates, then recommences the lovemaking. As the heat in the bedroom builds, the rain outside grows heavier, drumming on the roof like erotic African drums and providing generous cover for their moans.

A drop of water splashes onto Robert's face. He starts, then pulls away from Pamela.

"Christ! Is that what I think it is?"

"Hmm?" She continues kissing him.

Robert looks up. The ceiling starts to leak more forcefully. "I thought you said you were getting the roof fixed when I was away."

She looks blankly at him. "I . . . must have forgotten."

"Jesus, Pamela. What've you been doing?"

He climbs out of bed, pulls on his track-suit pants, and storms out of the room, while Pamela pulls the saucepan out from under the bed and limply holds it under the leak.

Robert huffs and puffs down the hall with the ladder. He positions it under the manhole in the ceiling and climbs up. He bangs at the manhole cover, violently dislodging a faceful of cobwebs and dust. "Shit! This bloody thing!"

At a loss, Pamela hovers at the bottom of the ladder while he pulls himself up into the ceiling. "Can I do anything?"

He doesn't answer. She can hear him swearing and cursing under the roof. He climbs down the ladder, pushes past her, and goes into the laundry with Pamela following him. She watches as he angrily raids the cupboards for plastic buckets and towels.

"I'm sorry Robert. I'm sure I . . . I mean, I didn't mean to forget. I mean, what with the kids, and work, you know . . ."

He ignores her and heads back up the ladder.

She calls up to him, "Has it ever occurred to you that I've been . . . *busy?*"

Returning to the bedroom, she goes to slam the door, before remembering the sleeping children. So she closes it quietly and sticks her tongue out at the ceiling, instead.

The More Things
Change . . .

The best part of the morning has been swallowed up by the time Pamela has seen everybody off to work and school, rung Dynamite Roof and Plumbing, done the washing up from breakfast, swept the kitchen floor, tidied up the toy box, hung out the wash, showered, and dressed. Finally, she stands at her desk and switches on the ancient computer. She presses some keys, stands back, and waits.

After much frustration she finds her way into the word-processing program and types a heading: THE MODERN WOMAN. Then she stares at the screen. For lack of any better ideas, she starts typing Deirdre's immortal words: "Now that we've bullied the guys into changing the sheets and leaving the toilet seat down, what do we really want?"

A very good question, Deirdre, Pamela thinks. Unfortunately, the answer is far from evident. She starts doodling on a pad. *What do we really want?*

A blast of commercial radio heralds the arrival of the Dynamite Roof and Plumbing crew. As they start work, Pamela wonders whether dynamite would actually have been the quieter option. She closes the study window, but the thumping and banging and whistling and yelling transmit very effectively through the ceiling. She seeks refuge in the kitchen and makes herself a peanut-butter sandwich.

Dynamite Roof and Plumbing pack up and leave Pamela in peace exactly three minutes before the kids come home from school. The noise-making baton is passed without a stumble to Douglas and Stacy, who are in mid-argument as they come through the door. Their high-pitched bickering is interspersed with floor thumping and door slamming.

Pamela sticks her head out of the study and yells out her mother's age-old threat: "If you two aren't quiet, I'll knock your heads together!"

Surprised by such an old-fashioned concept, Stacy and Douglas pause momentarily. Stacy dishes out one last dose of abuse, retreats to her bedroom, slams the door, and turns her music up loud. Its dull thud, joined seconds later by the barrage of Douglas's violent video games, is marginally less distracting than full-scale warfare. Pamela tries to settle down and concentrate. Soon she becomes irritated by a constant, rhythmic scratching noise. She glances across at Rupert, who sits at a miniature desk in the corner, deeply absorbed in coloring in a jungle scene. She is amazed at how much noise one box of crayons can make.

Focusing on the screen, she starts typing the first paragraph for the fifth time, but after a few moments she senses she is being watched. She turns around to find Rupert standing behind her, clutching his drawing book and a red crayon.

"I need a giraffe."

Pamela hesitates, then relents. She takes the proffered crayon and attempts a giraffe, which turns out to resemble a dog with a very long neck, due to the fact that she is using Brandy as a model. Rupert watches her efforts with a critical eye. They are interrupted by the telephone, but she keeps drawing as she picks up the phone with her spare hand.

"Hello? . . . Oh, Ben . . ."

She snaps the crayon.

"How are you? . . . Last night? . . . No, that's all right, it's just that I was . . . busy."

Rupert gazes steadily at her as she speaks. She turns away from him and lowers her voice.

"No, actually it's not really a good time. I'm . . . in a meeting. I'm not sure. . . . Sorry. Can I get back to you? . . . Oh, no, I don't . . ." She reaches for a pen and scribbles down his number, Rupert all the while quietly observing her. "Okay. 'Bye."

She slips Ben's number into the desk drawer and notices something glinting there. She reaches in and pulls out a packet of cigarettes, a lighter, and a tiny enameled ashtray. She smirks cynically at her find. "I gave up years ago!"

The door swings open and Douglas barges into the room, glaring accusingly at Pamela. "What did you do with my tool kit?"

Pamela spins around, concealing her discovery under the mouse pad.

"What tool kit?"

"The one you gave me, dummy."

She turns back to her work, which has become somewhat

difficult due to the lumpy mouse pad. She tries some random typing to look busy. "I didn't do anything with your tool kit, Douglas."

Douglas scowls. "Well, where is it? I need it."

"I don't know. Have you looked in your room?"

"It was on the floor. Under some stuff. You must have moved it."

Pamela stops typing and turns to face him. "I haven't touched your tool kit, Douglas."

He glares at her and turns away, muttering under his breath. "Bet you did, dumbhead."

She calls him back cheerfully. "Oh, and Douglas?"

He turns back sourly. "What?"

She smiles. "My name is Pamela. Apparently you have the right to call me 'Mum.' If you ever address me as 'dummy,' 'dumbhead,' or 'stupid' again, I guarantee you won't have any trouble finding your tool kit. Got it?"

Cowed by the force in her voice, Douglas nods, then backs away and closes the door. Pamela looks to Rupert. He smiles approvingly.

Stacy is sprawled on her bed with her head in her English folder. Music thumps from the ghetto blaster on her bedside table. Pamela opens the door and shouts across the room, "*Do you think you could turn that down a bit?*"

Stacy raises her eyes to the ceiling, reaches over, and turns the music down minimally. "Okay?"

Stacy returns to her work, while Pamela hovers in the doorway, wondering what it is that has Stacy so absorbed. "What are you doing?"

"Stream of consciousness."

Pamela's interest is sparked. "You like writing?"

Stacy shrugs. "It's okay."

Captivated, Pamela watches Stacy for a moment, then tentatively ventures into the room. "Stacy, can I ask you something?"

Stacy rolls her eyes and turns off the music. "I don't smoke. I don't drink and I can't afford drugs."

Pamela sits down on the end of the bed. Stacy pulls herself to the other end of the bed, bracing herself for a parental lecture.

"What would you say you want out of life?"

"What?"

"Well, what do you want to be . . . when you're older?"

Stacy groans. "Not this again. I don't know. Whatever I decide when I get there, I suppose. Do we have to panic yet?"

"But do you feel like you could do anything?"

Stacy nods coolly. "Sure. If I want to."

"What about getting married? Having children?"

"Not if they turn out anything like Douglas."

Pamela smiles. "Stacy, do you think life would be easier if you'd been born a boy?"

Stacy turns up her nose. "With all those dangly bits flopping around? Get real!"

Pamela laughs and rises from the bed.

As she reaches the door, Stacy calls after her, "Hey, Mum!"

Pamela tenses. She thought she'd successfully dealt with the anal-sex issue, and she dreads to think what today's topic is. She turns timidly.

Stacy fixes her with a solemn look. "Don't quote me."

She reaches over and turns her music back on. Pamela is dismissed.

159

The noise of the television filters into the study as Pamela types at full speed. Owing to the pair of purple ear muffs she found in the desk drawer, and which she cleverly realized were not intended for skiing, she doesn't hear Robert enter the room. He glances briefly at her work, then heads for the old armchair in the corner.

"Busy?"

Surprised, she jumps. He loosens his tie and sinks heavily into the chair.

She can't ignore this obvious display of exhaustion. "Bad day?"

Robert shakes his head and exhales loudly. "We lost the—"

"Huh?" Pamela remembers the ear muffs and whips them off, then pulls out the cotton-wool balls she stuffed in her ears earlier.

Her attention now gained, Robert wearily resumes. "We lost the town houses. Nathan and Trennery won the tender."

She tries her best to empathize, though she has no idea what he is talking about. "Oh, no. I'm sorry. That's terrible. Here, let me save this."

She turns back to the keyboard and presses a combination of keys. The machine gives an elongated beep and the screen goes blank.

She freezes. "Shit! Shit! Shit! This bloody machine." She thumps it. "How am I meant to work with this piece of *crap?*"

Robert winces. "Hey, lighten up. Can't be that bad. You've got a backup, haven't you?"

She shakes her head forlornly. "That's a whole day's work down the drain!"

Robert opens his arms to her. "Come here."

Pamela's anger softens and she crumples onto his lap while

he kisses her comfortingly. She manages a smile. "I've got to get a new computer."

Robert plants a kiss on her nose. "We'll see."

She regards him, bemused. "I wasn't asking your permission, Rob."

He strokes her hair. "Frankly, I don't see why you need a new computer just because you forgot to back up. That thing's good enough for your purposes, isn't it?"

She tenses. "What do you mean by that?"

"Nothing. I just don't know why suddenly you're getting so hysterical over it."

She can't believe her ears. "It's my work, isn't it?"

"I know. I know it is."

He reaches for her and she pulls away.

"Don't patronize me, Rob."

"I wasn't patronizing you!"

She scrutinizes him."You don't take my work seriously, do you?"

A look of annoyance crosses his face. "Oh, no, here we go."

Something in Robert's expression propels Pamela back into the past. In a split-second, memories of times gone by flash through her mind. University days, arguments in the refectory, debates in the bar, Sunday afternoon discussions in the kitchen over endless cups of tea served in cracked mugs, with slices of homemade banana cake. She remembers losing most of the arguments, and she also remembers backing down a lot to keep the peace.

At first she'd assumed that Robert did in fact know everything about most things, and she had been full of admiration for his vast knowledge and absolute certainty, until gradually it dawned on her that he just expounded his opinions with more confidence than she did, and that he never gave credence to her ideas unless they happened to be shared by one of his mates. Her admiration had turned to frustration, and after a while she learned not to argue points with him at all, even when she knew she was right. Over the intervening years the finer dynamics of their relationship have faded in her memory, but now everything is coming back to her, along with a rapidly growing knot in her stomach.

"You never thought I was as smart as you, did you?"

"Come on, Pam, don't be silly."

"*Stupid*, don't you mean?"

Robert flares, his face snarling. "Jesus! Give it a rest, can't you? I haven't got the energy."

He gets up and heads for the door.

She stares after him in recognition, as if she's seen a ghost. "My God, you haven't changed."

He barks back at her, "Should I have?"

Pamela shakes her head, the anger swelling inside her. It's obvious nobody has ever bullied this guy into anything. "Just out of interest, when was the last time *you* changed the sheets?"

Robert is struck dumb, failing to see the logic.

In a fury, in the kitchen, she scrapes the burned bits off a piece of blackened toast, puts the kettle on, then opens the cupboard for her packet of Tim-Tams. She finds it . . . empty.

With a plate of Vegemite toast and a cup of coffee in hand, she sweeps through the living room, with Douglas and Rupert watching as she enters her study and slams the door soundly behind her.

Having witnessed Pamela's stormy exit, Stacy joins her brothers in the living room, and they all look to Robert with concern. He tries to cover.

"No drama," he comments. "Mum just needs some time to herself."

Now Pamela sits glumly in front of the computer screen, her feet up on the chair and her arms wrapped around her knees. *The Modern Woman.* Huh! What a myth. She stares at the blank screen, still bubbling with anger. How is it that men can be so bloody infuriating? She hasn't felt such turbulent emotions for a long time—not since her last relationship, anyway.

She's angry at Robert, but she's more angry at herself. How could Pamela Dickson have maintained the status quo for so many years? How did she let him get away with it? She supposes she has the benefit of more experience, for she has certainly had to deal with worse than Robert over the years. But to have to seek his approval to buy a half-decent computer for her work? To be patted on the head like a poodle! She's earned good money, for God's sake.

She tries to rationalize Robert's position. He's an old-fashioned kind of guy. He probably handles the finances of the household, and he probably contributes the principal income. But to treat Pamela like that . . . to be so patronizing. Just like her father. No, he wasn't patronizing, exactly; it's just that he would unthinkingly and systematically disregard his wife's opinions. Pamela once asked her mother how she had put up with it, and her mother admitted that, after thirty years of marriage, it does start eating into your soul a tiny bit. Pamela swore it would never happen to her. Her mother had replied, "I'm sure it won't, dear. You're far too selfish." Well, maybe she is.

Her eyes go to the desk drawer, knowing full well what lies within. She hesitates, then slowly pulls the drawer open and reaches for the hidden packet of cigarettes, which she opens, to find one remaining cigarette. She brings the packet to her nose,

163

closes her eyes, and breathes deeply. She tells herself firmly that it won't make her feel any better, and besides, she's sure she wouldn't be allowed to smoke in the house. Sighing, she returns the packet to the back of the drawer. As she closes it, she glimpses the scrap of paper with Ben Monroe's phone number on it. She picks it up and contemplates it, then sighs ruefully, betting he changes the sheets *and* leaves the toilet seat down.

164

Morning sunshine streams onto Pamela, now slumped over her desk, asleep.

Robert enters, bearing a fresh cup of coffee, and he awakens her gently. "'Morning."

Pamela pulls herself up, rubbing her neck back into shape. She feels like shit. She takes the coffee and breathes in the aroma. "Thanks."

Robert hovers awkwardly, glancing at her scattered notes. "So, how's it going?"

She turns back to the keyboard, sliding Ben's number under some papers. "Okay."

Robert hesitates, then leans over and kisses the top of her head. "Rupert hasn't got any lunch."

She wraps a cheese sandwich and packs it with some juice and an apple into Rupert's lunchbox. She buckles it into his little backpack and hands it to him, then straightens his Superman sloppy-joe, which he has managed to put on by himself— albeit backward.

Douglas power-blades through the kitchen. "See you!"

Pamela wearily calls after him. "Douglas, can't you wait for your sister for once?"

The door slams in response. Robert takes a last mouthful of

toast, grabs his keys, and kisses Pamela good-bye. She wipes the resulting residue of marmalade off her cheek.

"Have you seen Stacy yet?"

He shakes his head and takes Rupert's hand. "Come on, sport."

Rupert trots after his dad, his backpack trailing on the floor.

Pamela calls out loudly. "*Stacy!*" She knocks on Stacy's door and enters to find Stacy still in bed, buried under the bed-clothes. "Stacy? You're going to be late. Are you getting up?"

Stacy's lying face down in her pillow. Pamela gently lifts up the corner of the comforter. Stacy turns over, her face red from crying.

"Stacy, what is it?"

Stacy starts sobbing. "What do you think?"

Pamela rifles through the bathroom cabinet and comes up with an armful of sanitary napkins and tampons for all occasions, then unloads them onto Stacy's bed. Stacy stares like a frightened rabbit at them. As does Pamela. She's totally unprepared to handle the situation.

She tries the matter-of-fact approach. "Right . . . well, these are what people use. You've got the pads, which you just put in your underpants. They've got sticky bits underneath so they stay where they're supposed to. Very simple to use, and these ones have got quite a nice smell. Boy, you should have seen them in my day. You had to use safety pins and a belt contraption, God, don't I sound old? Anyway, they make them pretty high-tech these days, but if you want to go swimmimg or whatever, like in all the ads on TV, then tampons are more convenient. But you have to remember to change them every few hours or you could get toxic shock syndrome, which can kill you. To tell you the truth, they can be a bit tricky at first. I remember going through a whole tub of Vaseline before I got one in. . . ."

Stacy looks as if she is going to have a breakdown, and Pamela racks her brain for something more appropriately motherly and reassuring to say.

"Really, you should be . . . pleased. It means you're becoming a woman. Most girls would be thrilled about it."

Stacy scrutinizes a heavy-flow tampon. "I think the whole thing stinks."

Pamela can't help nodding in agreement.

In the meantime, the kitchen tap is dripping onto a stack of dirty breakfast dishes and the floor remains unswept. As her magazine deadline looms, the housework slides down the scale of Pamela's priorities and she wonders how she is supposed to cope without cleaning help. She makes a mental note to broach the subject with Robert when he gets home, then shudders at the thought.

She types away with gathering momentum, gradually getting a handle on the article . . . until she is interrupted.

"*Mum!*"

With trepidation, she knocks on the bathroom door, around which Stacy pokes her head.

"I can't work out what's what." She brandishes a miniature diagram of the female anatomy.

Pamela leans close to study it and nods. "You see, this is like they've cut you down the middle. And this is where it's supposed to go. But it doesn't really help. You've just got to kind of feel your way."

Stacy is disheartened.

Pamela is at a loss. "Uh . . . would you like me to—"

Horrified, Stacy slams the door in her face.

Pamela's concentration is shot and she returns to the dinosaur computer to delete the last paragraph and press Save. Restless, she glances at her watch, then returns to the still-closed bathroom door. "You okay in there?"

There's no answer. She opens the door tentatively, to be met by the tragic picture of Stacy sitting on the edge of the bathtub in defeat, tears streaming down her face. "I can't do it. It hurts."

Pamela's heart goes out to her, suddenly understanding why her mother had wanted sons. She sits next to her and puts an arm around her. "There's no hurry, honey. Why don't you just stick to the pads this time?"

She hands her a packet of super-absorbent sanitary napkins. Stacy pulls one out of the packet and holds it up. She screws up her face. "Surfboards!"

By noon Stacy is lying on the couch, wrapped up in Pamela's dressing gown, hugging a hot-water bottle to her tummy and feeling extremely sorry for herself. A hospital soap is playing on the television. Pamela brings her a tray with a mug of hot chocolate and toast with sprinkles. Stacy smiles the limp gratitude of an invalid, then turns back to the TV. Pamela, drawn in by the violins, perches on the arm of the couch. "What's happening?"

Stacy shushes her, then whispers a hurried explanation. "Dr. Hearnshaw is just about to tell Danni that her unborn baby that she is having to replace her last baby which was stolen by her stepsister is HIV-positive because Nathan her husband's been having an affair with Trisha Dubois who was raped when she was sixteen by Alex Figaro, the son of her mother's boss who was a junky. That was before he became a priest."

Pamela nods intelligently. She whispers back. "I remember when he was born."

"Who?"

"Alex Figaro. Except he's not a real Figaro. His mother died of leukemia when he was a baby, and his father couldn't bear to keep him because he blamed him for his mother's death, so he sold him to Reynaldo Figaro the lingerie baron, who was sterile and couldn't have an heir of his own."

Stacy is impressed. "Wow! This show must be really old."

The credits roll on a ponderous close-up of Dr. Hearnshaw, the dreadful news teetering on his lips. Stacy switches to *Oprah*.

Pamela glances at the time, knowing that she really should get back to work. "I'm just going down the shops. Won't be long. Okay?"

"Okay."

Pamela picks up her keys, then hovers in the doorway. "Are you sure? You'll be all right?"

Stacy appreciates Pamela's concern, but she covers with a brusque reply. "Go!"

Midlife Crisis 12

Pamela pushes open the stiff wrought-iron gate to a terrace house and walks up the path. She hesitates at the door, wondering what the hell she is doing. It's not too late to turn around and forget the whole thing. But she knocks on the door to spite herself. She promptly changes her mind and turns around. As she fumbles with the gate, the door opens.

"Hey. I thought I'd been stood up."

Pamela turns and smiles at Ben. "Hello."

"Come in."

She hesitates, then approaches the doorway. She stops. "I don't have long."

Ben nods sympathetically. "Do you think you could manage a cup of coffee? I've got a quick-boil kettle."

He smiles. She gulps. "Actually, I don't think I should be here at all."

He looks frankly at her. "You don't?"

Reluctantly she meets his gaze. "No. I don't."

They stand in the doorway, face to face, with an attraction so strong that the kiss is inevitable. It explodes into a wave of hungry passion and they fall against the hallway wall in a frenzied embrace. Ben kicks the front door shut.

It is midafternoon by the time the earth has stopped moving. They lie across the bed, entwined and exhausted. Pamela can't remember ever having had such good first-time sex. Maybe it's just her imagination, but she doesn't think it was just sex. It felt bigger than that, like a meeting of the souls. She mentally slaps herself across the face. *Cut it out, Pamela, it was just good sex.*

"Hungry?"

She nods vigorously.

Ben extricates himself from her naked body. "Great. Don't move."

She watches him pull on his shirt and goes tingly all over. Lying back in the bed, she listens to the glorious rattle of pots and pans coming from the kitchen, delighted to note that he cooks in this life as well. Rolling over, she tidies up the scattered packet of condoms that has fallen on the floor, then drops them into the bedside drawer. She can't help noticing the glint of a gold photo frame lying half-buried under assorted toiletries. She knows she shouldn't, but her curiosity gets the better of her. She pulls out a picture of a much younger Ben and a pretty young woman with flame-red hair. The photo is signed "All My Love, Sophie."

Pamela recognizes her as a younger version of the woman at the window that rainy night at Ben's apartment. In the other life. The life where Sophie didn't get hit by a drunken driver.

The love of his life. Marriage, kids, matching pajamas . . . She feels a pang of sadness for this Ben who missed out on that happiness and who clearly is hurting still, then returns the picture to the drawer.

Standing at the window, she is pensive. She can hear Ben whistling as he cooks, and she can smell something wonderful coming from the kitchen. She looks across the road to a primary school. A bell rings and the playground fills with kids running and yelling and playing football. She watches one boy as he climbs to the top of the climbing equipment, beats his chest, lets out a scream, then hurls himself to the ground. He is bold and brash and loud. Just like Douglas.

Ben pushes open the bedroom door, bearing an omelette and salad and a bottle of wine. "I hope you'll drink Spanish wine. It's all I've got."

He stops. Pamela has gone.

She types methodically and without inspiration. She can't help glancing at the phone as she types. Finally, she reaches out and pulls it off the hook, cursing herself for her weakness, and is startled by a low knock on the door.

Robert pokes his head in, a bedsheet bundled in his arms. "Er . . . will I change the top sheet as well?"

Pamela has some trouble looking him in the eye. "What? . . . Oh, yes, please."

"And they can both fit in the washing machine together?"

She nods, then turns back to her work.

"Do we have matching pillow cases?"

"Pardon?"

"If I'm putting on the blue sheets, will the flowery pillow cases do?"

Moved by his good, if inept, intentions, Pamela tries to nod and smile encouragingly. He grins, adjusts his halo, then closes the door.

Pamela pulls out the scrap of paper with Ben's number on it. She turns it over and over between her fingers, watching his name come and go. Sighing, she crumples it up and drops it into the bin.

It's after midnight when she wearily pulls on her koala T-shirt and crawls into bed. Robert rolls toward her and starts making sexual overtures. She doesn't have the energy or the inclination to reciprocate.

Robert senses her lack of enthusiasm. "Is it finished?"

She freezes. "Is what finished?"

"The article."

"Oh. . . . Mmm."

She turns away and closes her eyes as he props himself up on one elbow and addresses her back. "So the pressure's off? Because, it's just that I sort of asked Geoff and Janine for dinner. Tomorrow night."

Pamela opens her eyes. Just what she needs—a stint in the role of hostess with the mostest. "How 'sort of'?"

"Completely 'sort of.' But nothing fancy, I said. That'll be okay, won't it?"

She musters a nod and Robert smiles with relief, kissing the back of her neck. He continues nuzzling her until he senses she's asleep. Disappointed, he lies back. Pamela opens her eyes and stares into the darkness.

Hours later, she's still awake and listening to Robert's sonorous snoring, her head in a turmoil. What's so wrong with her that she manages to make a mess of every life she leads?

What kind of cruel practical joke is this, anyway? She's finally got the man and the family she's been yearning for since forever, and she's committed adultery at the first opportunity. How pathetic is that?

She slips out of bed, pulls on her gown, creeps downstairs to the sideboard in the living room, and opens the cupboard where the family photograph albums are kept in chronological order. She finds the post-marriage albums and pores over them for a clue. Some clue as to the truth of the marriage. Like an amnesia victim in a daytime soap, she grapples to fill in the gaping holes in her life with Robert. How have they dealt with the passing years, and how well has the relationship endured?

173

They look happy enough in the photos, but then photos are like that. A blazing row doesn't quite qualify as a photo opportunity. She notes that there don't seem to be as many photos since Rupert was born. Is that significant? Or is it simply that when you have three kids, you don't have much time left for photography?

She flips backward through the album, reaching a series of herself eight months pregnant with Stacy. She stares and stares at the pictures. How could that be her? What could it possibly feel like? Had she been frightened? She traces the outline of her bulging stomach with her finger. She puts her hand to her own stomach and tries to imagine a memory of it. But she can't remember. The simple truth is that she was in India researching an article on immolation at the time. Single, and zero months pregnant. She turns back to a photo of Pamela and Robert taken at their wedding as they cut the five-tiered marzipan-covered cake. Robert's hand encloses Pamela's. They are both smiling radiantly.

The sun's just starting to tint the sky when she drops her

gown onto the floor and crawls back into bed. Miraculously, Robert's snoring has ceased and she snuggles close to him. He stirs, resting a hand on her thigh. She puts her hand on his, then falls asleep.

In the morning, in his newly assumed role of house husband, Robert volunteers to make Rupert's lunch while Pamela prints out her article. She plugs in the obsolete printer and switches it on. Nothing. She wiggles the cord, thumps the machine, and threatens a one-way trip to the rubbish dump. It responds by blinking and beeping into action. She searches the filing shelf for some printing paper, and spots an open ream under a pile of manila folders. Pulling it out, she dislodges the folders, which drop to the floor. Stooping down to retrieve them, she finds among them a folder of memorabilia, including two more copies of her "Cadet of the Year" photo, her university degree certificate, and a letter. She unfolds the letter. It has been folded and refolded many times, has a tear along one edge, and a coffee stain on the top-right corner. The header is: NATIONAL ASSOCIATED PUBLICATIONS. She scans the letter:

> *Dear Mrs. Dickson,*
> *After much consideration . . . pleased to offer . . . full-time position . . . senior feature writer . . .*

Pamela stares at what is a very impressive job offer.

"Are you going in to work?"

She jumps. Stacy stands at the door, dressed for school, as Pamela folds up the letter and slips it back into the folder. "I've . . . just got to print this thing out."

"Can you give me a ride? I think I've missed the bus."

"Sure."

Pamela regards Stacy with sympathy.

"You going to be okay? You sure you want to go back to-day?"

Stacy nods ambivalently. She walks across the room with an exaggerated waddle, as if astride an invisible horse. She turns to Pamela. "Can you tell?"

Pamela shakes her head emphatically. "No way."

They share a smile.

At the National Consolidated Press building, she pushes through the revolving doors and hurries over to the security desk, to be greeted warmly by the large female security guard. "'Morning, Pamela. How are you today?"

Pamela looks blankly to the guard. "'Morning . . ." Her eyes flick to the name tag on the desk. ". . . Adriana. How are you? . . . Uh, look, could you get this up to Deirdre Reynolds?"

"Sure. Not a problem. Can you pop her name on it?"

Adriana pulls the pen from her breast pocket. Pamela grabs it and scribbles the details onto the envelope.

"Flying visit, huh?"

Pamela turns to find herself face to face with Ben. Exactly what she was hoping to avoid. "Oh . . . yes, it is, actually."

"You're good at those."

"Look, I'm sorry about . . ."

She hands the article to Adriana and moves away. Adriana clears her throat loudly and raises her eyebrows at Pamela, who is disconcerted by her lewd insinuations.

Ben smiles. "I think you've made off with her pen."

Pamela registers that she is indeed still clutching the security-desk pen and returns it, mumbling an apology.

Ben waits for her. "Can we talk?"

She reluctantly shakes her head. "I'm sorry, Ben."

She turns to go and he touches her arm, lightly but urgently. "Was it something I did? I said?"

"No! God, no."

"Then what's the matter? Am I just too good to be true?"

He smiles, hoping for a playful rejoinder, but she simply looks at him, torn. If only he knew.

He sighs. "Look, I haven't done this for a while. Just tell me you're not interested . . . and I'll leave you alone."

"I'm sorry, Ben, I can't explain. I just can't see you. It's . . . complicated."

He frowns. "Is there someone else?"

She wishes she could tell him the half of it. But at that moment there's an agitated knocking on the window by the revolving door. They both turn to see Stacy standing outside in the forecourt. She mouths impatiently to Pamela, "Come on, Mum!"

Ben turns back to Pamela. "*Mum?*"

Pamela grimaces. "It's not what you think."

Ben takes a moment. "What I *think* is that you're somebody's mother. And probably, by the way you're behaving, married to somebody's father. Am I warm?"

She shrugs. "I guess so."

"You *guess* so!"

"All right, yes."

"Is that all?"

She shakes her head morosely. "Three kids, a mortgage, a dog, two goldfish, and a husband. But it's not really me, and I honestly don't know how long it will last."

Ben stares at her, appalled. "Is this how you tell your readers to keep the marriage alive?"

"You don't understand . . . I can explain."

"Can you?"

Pamela turns to Stacy, who is gesticulating impatiently. Ben waits. She turns back to him. "Would you believe . . . I'm having a midlife crisis?"

She tries to smile. Ben looks at her dryly. He turns and walks away, his footsteps echoing on the vast marble floor.

After dropping Stacy at school, Pamela can't bear the thought of returning to the empty house. She finds herself yearning for a friend, and not just any friend.

Terri opens her front door, to find Pamela on her doorstep. "Hey!"

Pamela's smile is fragile. "Hey."

A day-glo clad cyclist whizzes past them as they power-walk through the local park. Terri sports the latest lycra gear, complete with Velcro-attached hand weights. Pamela makes do with the old pair of jogging shoes Terri's found in the wardrobe.

Terri takes a swig from her water bottle, then hands it to Pamela. "You know, I can't even remember the last time we did this together. I think you must've been pregnant with Douglas."

Pamela is appalled. "God, really? That long?"

"How is the little treasure?"

Pamela grimaces. "He might improve with age."

"You've been saying that since he was three weeks old!"

"Have I?"

Pamela's deeply grateful that she's missed out on the intervening years. Bringing up Douglas would be enough to drive anybody mad. "So, how are you and . . ."

"Daniel? Oh, you know . . . Sex—great. Conversation—who cares!" Terri grins. "I mean, he's not for keeps, but he's a good boy. Anyway, I'm off to Italy in June, so I guess it'll be *say-onara,* baby."

"*Arrivederci.*"

Pamela's amazed at how happy Terri seems as a single woman. There's no perceptible difference in her sense of well-being from the time when she had Leonard and Otto. How did she get born with such a goddamned positive attitude?

"Terri? Why have I got such a crappy job?"

Terri raises her eyes to the heavens. "What are you talking about? The hottest women's glossy in the country?"

"But it's rubbish. Do you read it?"

"Avidly. Every time I go to the doctor."

Pamela shakes her head. "It's everything I hate. You know, I was offered something decent, something worthwhile . . ."

"Oh, no, you don't still think about that bloody job offer, do you? How many years ago are we talking about?"

"But why did I turn it down? It was Robert, wasn't it?"

Terri stops and looks in surprise at Pamela. "What are you talking about? You didn't even tell Robert. If I remember correctly, you decided to postpone saving the world to stay home with the kids. I think you considered that worthwhile. Besides, you reckoned you could make better money, part-time, writing . . . rubbish."

Pamela absorbs this. "So I could have taken the job."

Terri groans. "Do you ever stop? Honestly, Pamela, you've got to get hold of yourself. You can't keep chasing your tail like this, looking for the life that got away."

Italian Porridge 13

Terri's words do the rounds of Pamela's head as she scrubs the soap scum off the bathtub. As much as Pamela hates to admit it, Terri is absolutely right. It's a question of commitment. She has to commit to the life she's in. And for better or worse, she seems to be firmly planted in this one. She stands up from the bathtub, massaging her aching back, and watches Rupert as he painstakingly collects the hairs out of the plug hole. Like a little blond angel sent from heaven to make her feel guilty.

Having made up her mind to embrace her situation and banish all lingering thoughts of Ben Monroe, not to mention past career opportunities, she vacuums the living room with a determinedly positive attitude. Rupert helps her by running in front of her and moving the cushions.

She changes the beds and collects the dirty wash from the children's rooms, then fetches the wash basket from the master bedroom. She starts sorting the wash into various piles, until she realizes all is quiet.

"Rupert?"

She looks into the den, the kitchen, the hallway. Rupert is nowhere to be seen.

"Rupert!"

She feels a tiny pang of worry and calls again, louder. "*Rupert!*"

She hears a door open. Rupert emerges from the bathroom, the sound of the toilet flushing behind him. He solemnly pulls up his trousers, then looks triumphantly at Pamela. Pamela can't help smiling.

She starts loading the washing machine while Rupert finishes sorting the clothes. He's energetically shaking out a pile of jeans when a handful of coins falls onto the floor. He gets down on his hands and knees to retrieve them. "What's this?"

Pamela is busy untangling a bra and underpants.

Rupert insists. "What *is* it?"

She turns and focuses on the object Rupert is offering up to her, wide-eyed. It takes her a moment to recognize it, lying there in a little child's hand. It's an empty condom wrapper. Suddenly, she can feel her newfound positive attitude draining through her feet.

Violently chopping the carrots with the sharpest knife in the kitchen, Pamela is heedless of the bits that fly off the counter and onto the floor. The children are locked up with the television and a frozen pizza.

Robert comes into the kitchen, picks his way through the carrot cuttings, and reaches to get some champagne glasses out of the cupboard. "Smells great."

The doorbell rings.

Robert squeezes her waist. "Now, try not to pick a fight with Geoff, okay? At least not in the first five minutes." He grins and kisses her on the cheek.

She keeps chopping madly. "Is it Janine?"

Robert is still smiling as he turns in the doorway. "Is what Janine?"

"Or Harriet, maybe? I mean, it makes sense. She's not exactly nubile, but she's nice and young."

Robert's smile fades. The doorbell rings again.

"What are you talking about?"

Pamela drops the knife and turns to him. "It is. Isn't it? You're actually fucking the baby-sitter."

Robert has gone pale. "No. Of course not! Don't be ridiculous."

Pamela raises her brow. "Well, who, then?"

He glances in the direction of the front door. "Do you think we could talk about this later?"

"I'd rather know now. Who is she? Who's the other woman in our lives? Tell me, Robert."

Robert meets her gaze evenly. "There's no other woman. I swear."

"Oh, please, give me a break! Is that what your little business trip to Melbourne was all about?"

He shakes his head, expressionless. "Pam, believe me. I'm telling you. There's no one."

Scraping out the saucepan noisily, Pamela dollops a mass of gray, stodgy rice onto a plate and plunks it in front of Robert, who attempts a gracious smile. She takes her seat and drains her glass of wine in one gulp. Janine is busy spreading her napkin on her lap, as if her life depends on it, having picked up on the domestic disharmony as soon as she came through the front door.

Geoffrey Ballodero, oblivious to the dangerous ambience, dives enthusiastically into his meal. "Mmm . . . Great, Pammy. I mean it. Very tasty." He takes another mouthful and washes it down with a gulp of wine. "Rob told me you'd been branching out in the old cuisine lately. So, what do you call this little creation?"

Janine throws a warning glance at him. "Risotto." She takes a mouthful herself and struggles to swallow.

Geoffrey raises his eyebrows. "Very . . . interesting. Sort of like Italian porridge, is it, Pammy?"

"Honey, don't."

"What?"

"You know she hates you calling her that."

Pamela looks at Geoff and regards him for a few moments. She smiles warmly. "So, Geoff, I see you still chew with your mouth open."

Geoff stops mid-mouthful and Robert tenses.

Janine is astonished by Pamela's rudeness, but she tries to make light of it. "Oh, my God, does he? I must've got used to it. Ten years and he's barely house-trained." She reaches over and squeezes his hand lovingly. "But what can I do?"

Robert tries to help. "Obedience school?"

Janine laughs a little too loudly. "Grooming and deportment?"

Pamela smiles. "Shock treatment?"

Geoff raises his hands in self-defense. "Hey! Ceasefire! Sorry, people. I'm an old dog. I'm afraid you'll have to love me or leave me."

Pamela smiles sweetly. "Gee, I know what I'd do." And she looks pointedly at Robert.

Somehow the guests have managed to consume the inedible risotto with admirable grace, and now the sink is filled with brown, soupy water as Pamela scrubs the bottom of a terminally blackened saucepan with intensity. She doesn't feel betrayed so much as completely and utterly pissed off. Perhaps if he'd crumpled to the floor and begged forgiveness she would have had some compassion. But to lie barefacedly like that? What did he take her for?

A little voice inside her head interrupts to suggest that she is being a tad hypocritical. Hadn't she strayed from the marriage bed, just the other day? That doesn't count, she rejoins; *she* hadn't actually been married to him for more than thirteen years. Whereas he had been absolutely married to her. Pamela Dickson, at least. And apparently he thought he could get away with it. Cheating on Pamela Dickson, devoted wife and mother of his children, and household slave.

She ceases the rhythmic scrubbing, regards the saucepan blankly, then drops it into the flip-top rubbish bin. Geoff enters cheerfully. Pamela groans inwardly.

"Need some help there, Pammy?"

"No, thank you, Geoffrey."

He finds a tea towel and starts drying up anyway, while Pamela does her best to ignore his presence.

"So, who were you trying to convince in there? Them or yourself?"

She flicks him a look of annoyance. "What?"

She turns her attention to another saucepan and scrubs at

it with exaggerated intensity. Geoff moves up behind her, puts his lips to her neck, and murmurs in a low voice, "I'm sorry, I'm an old and disobedient dog. I just can't stay away."

Pamela drops the scourer into the water with a splash. He moves his lips to her ear and starts nibbling.

"I have to see you again. I'm going crazy. This is torture."

Stomach lurching, she wheels around to face him. Geoff looks deep into her eyes, pulls her to him, and kisses her. Completely flabbergasted, she steps backward and stammers, "What . . . do you think . . . you're doing?"

Geoff runs his hand through her hair, causing her skin to crawl. "I can't stand being apart, Pammy."

She stares at him, horrified. "I think you'd better go back inside."

He leans toward her and gives her a more gentle, lingering kiss. Flustered, she pulls away, just as Janine enters the kitchen. Janine gasps. "I don't believe it!"

Pamela looks away in humiliation.

Janine shakes her head in shock. "Geoff wielding a tea towel! Wonders never cease!"

Geoff limply picks up a glass and proceeds to dry it.

Pamela pulls off her rubber gloves. "Will you excuse me? I'm feeling sick. I think I'd better go and lie down. Sorry to be rude."

Janine's face fills with concern. "No, not at all! We'll finish off here. Won't we, kitchen-hand?"

Geoff nods reluctantly, following Pamela with his eyes as she leaves the room.

It's the truth; Pamela is really feeling ill. She's lying on the bed, nauseated. Devoted wife and mother. Huh! There she was, accusing Robert of infidelity, and all along it's been her—and with about the most repulsive man in the entire universe. Geoffrey Ballodero! In her wildest nightmares, she couldn't have predicted she'd come to that. How could she have sunk that low? She tries to block out the gruesome image of the two of them going at it . . . where? Hotel rooms? In the car? Here, while Robert was at work?

She hears Robert saying good-bye to Geoff and Janine. The front door closes and the lights are switched off. He climbs the stairs wearily and enters the bedroom. Sinking onto the end of the bed, he starts to unbutton his shirt mechanically.

"Well, that went well," he says, and he turns to Pamela, who lies there stiffly. "How can I convince you? What do I have to say?"

She turns away. "Nothing. It really doesn't matter."

Robert is clearly distressed. He drops his head in his hands. "What do you mean? Of course it matters. I'm not cheating on you! What makes you think . . ."

She shifts uncomfortably. "Nothing, Robert. I know you're not. Forget it. Can we just forget it?"

He stares at her, incredulous. "Christ! Things were just starting to work for us again. I know I haven't been the world's best husband. But I swear I haven't . . . with anyone . . . for ages."

This remark registers immediately with Pamela. "You *what?*"

"I swear. Not recently. You know that."

Robert rubs his brow exhaustedly, gets up, and goes into the bathroom, leaving Pamela in a state of horrified amazement.

After shaking out the lone cigarette from the packet, she takes it in her fingers and studies it under the yellow light of the streetlamp. The cold concrete of the curb seeps through her dressing gown to her backside, but that isn't the only part of her that feels numb. She puts the cigarette to her mouth and flicks on the lighter, trying to absorb the latest developments in what is rapidly appearing to be the farce of her life.

So, not only has Pamela been fooling around with Robert's oldest mate, but Robert, otherwise known as Mr. Right, has cheated on Pamela with God knows how many people for God knows how many years. Safe sex all round, no doubt. The perfect marriage.

She blows a lungful of angry smoke into the night air. If she could add up all the precious time she's wasted on wishing herself into this life, and what for? Geoffrey Ballodero! She shivers. All those miserable, self-indulgent nights of yearning and regret. All those bottles of gin and all that bloody Carole King. She sucks bitterly on the cigarette.

She hears the crunch of footsteps in the grass and braces herself for Robert's approach. She suspected he wasn't asleep when she slipped out of bed. He'd been too quiet. She wishes he'd just leave her alone; she really isn't in the mood for a heart-to-heart with a man she no longer knows.

He stops a few paces in front of her and regards the cigarette curiously. "You got another one of those?"

Surprised, Pamela shakes her head. Don't say he's a closet smoker, too. How deep can hypocrisy run in one family? She offers him the half-smoked cigarette. "It's stale."

He takes a drag, coughs like a teenager, hands it back to Pamela, then sits down next to her, but not too close. They sit there in silence. A dog barks in the distance.

Robert looks up at the night sky. "Remember how much we

used to smoke when we first met? God, we even used to roll our own."

Pamela does remember the blue packets of Drum and the slices of cucumber they used to stop them from drying out. "There were always bits of tobacco in the bed."

Robert laughs. "God, did we ever change the sheets in those days?"

Pamela can't help smiling. She stamps out the cigarette and kicks the butt onto the street. "Robert? . . ."

He turns to her. She looks up at the sky. "Are we staying together because of the children?"

He sucks in his breath. "Is that what you think?"

She shrugs. "Is there anything else left?"

Robert doesn't respond immediately but picks up a stick from the gutter and starts poking it into the soft bits of tar at his feet, using it to punctuate his thoughts. "I know we've run off the tracks. But I'm trying. And lately, I've felt there's hope. Something's changed. You seem . . . different."

He looks to Pamela who doesn't meet his eyes.

"I don't know what you want, Pam. But I want it back. Our marriage. Like it was in the beginning. I love you. I've always loved you."

Pamela looks away, not wanting him to see the tears in her eyes. How she used to dream of hearing those words from him. Now she just wants to go home.

When's Mummy Coming Home? 14

The alarm clock on Pamela's side of the bed goes off. She groans, slams it quiet, then buries herself under the bedding, loath to start the day.

Robert comes out of the bathroom and pulls on his jacket. He hesitates in the doorway, looking at the lump that is Pamela curled up under the covers. "See you."

"Mmm . . ." She listens for the front door to close before she lets herself drift back to sleep.

Douglas shakes her awake urgently. "Mum! *Mum!* Rupert's having another attack."

She surfaces from under the covers and blinks groggily at Douglas. He is obviously distressed, for once appearing like a vulnerable little boy.

"What?"

"He can't breathe!"

"*Who* can't breathe?"

"Rupert!"

Alarmed by Douglas's tone, she rolls out of bed, grabs her dressing gown, and hurries into the boys' room. Rupert is sitting in the middle of the floor in his pajamas. His face is chalk-white, his breathing is labored, and he is coughing and wheezing uncontrollably. Pamela lifts him onto his bed while Douglas stands at the door, watching, worried. She turns to him reassuringly. "It's all right, Douglas. You'll be late for school. Off you go. He'll be fine."

Hesitating, Douglas leaves, and Pamela turns back to Rupert. She's never seen an asthma attack before, but this doesn't look good. She offers him a glass of water, but he pushes it away in distress, struggling to breathe, looking to her, frightened. She racks her brain. She doesn't remember seeing any medication anywhere in the house, and Pamela Dickson never mentioned anything about asthma in the family, but then there was a lot she didn't mention. She tries the cupboards and drawers, panicked by Rupert's rasping gasps for air, before she turns to him urgently. "Where did we put your medicine, Rupert? Can you remember?"

He nods and points to the top of the bookshelf, where there sits a blue plastic box, which Pamela grabs and clicks open with relief. It is a nebulizer. She stares at the unfamiliar machine, the tube and mask and medication, and frantically scans the enclosed leaflet for a clue as to how it all works. But she can't find any instructions.

"Okay, Rupert, we're going to have to do this together. You know how to help Mummy, don't you?"

Rupert nods tearfully. Between coughs he picks up the vial of medication and holds it up to Pamela. She sees that she has to snap the top off. Then he takes the mask and shows her the compartment where the medication goes. She gets the idea and pours it all in, her hand trembling. Rupert picks up the tube that leads from the machine and starts screwing it into the bottom of the mask, his little fingers struggling. Pamela takes it from him and finishes the assembly. Then she plugs the machine in at the wall, while Rupert pulls the mask onto his face. She pulls the loose straps tight, switches the nebulizor on, and prays. The machine starts up noisily, the mask steams up, and Rupert begins to inhale the vapor. Within moments his breathing deepens and he stops coughing. Pamela strokes his head while his breathing normalizes.

191

"Good boy."

She swallows back her tears of relief.

His hand lying softly curled on the pillow, Rupert's cherubic face is finally calm in exhausted slumber. Pamela sits by his bed, painstakingly sewing an odd button onto the vacant spot that once was Kanga's eye. She isn't doing a very precise job—the eyes are uneven—but at least Kanga will soon be fully sighted.

She ties off the thread, leans over, and gently places Kanga on the pillow beside Rupert, gazing at his face, now flushed pink.

The doorbell rings and Brandy starts barking noisily. Rupert stirs but doesn't awaken.

Pamela grabs Brandy's collar and pulls him away from the front door. "Shh! Brandy! Good boy."

She opens the door and immediately regrets it when she sees Geoffrey Ballodero standing on the doorstep. His face is ashen, and his clothes creased. In fact, Pamela observes, he hasn't changed his outfit since the previous night.

"Geoffrey!"

"It's done."

He brushes past her and enters the house. Pamela closes the door with a sense of foreboding and follows him into the kitchen. "What's done?"

He leans against the wall and closes his eyes dramatically. "I left Janine—last night. I couldn't go on living a lie. She took it pretty badly. I tried . . . She doesn't know about . . . you."

He takes her by the shoulders, but Pamela pulls away impatiently. "Get off, Geoffrey. Go home."

He doesn't seem to have heard. "It's up to us now, Pammy. We can be together. Come away with me." He pulls her to him and starts groping her urgently.

She pushes him away and stares at him with incomprehension. "Come away? With you? Quite frankly, I can't imagine how I could've even . . ." Her face twists with revulsion. ". . . but do you seriously think there's a chance that I would leave this family for you? That I'd ever choose *you*?"

He stares at her, bewildered. "Well . . . yeah."

Just then the telephone rings. Pamela pounces on it, glad for the interruption, and she turns her back on Geoffrey.

"Hello? . . . Oh, Deirdre. Hi. . . . *Rewrite* it? . . . Yes, I know what the brief was, but the topic just isn't that simple. . . . Uh-huh . . . Uh-huh . . . Oh, I see, you want more of the same unadulterated moronic shit that your crappy magazine usually churns out. Well, maybe you should do the rewrite yourself. You'd be a natural!"

She slams the phone down furiously, oblivious to Geoffrey, who moves up behind her and wraps his arms around her.

"Come on, Pammy . . ." He plants his moist lips on her neck.

She sidesteps and elbows him soundly in the gut. "*No!*"

Followed by a sharp fist to the groin. Geoffrey doubles up in agony and hits the floor, looking to Pamela in shock.

She smiles down at him apologetically. "Sorry, Geoff, but I've never liked you."

He writhes on the floor, whimpering like a wounded dog.

Holding the front door open, she watches him shuffle out, still nursing his beloved groin. She closes the door firmly behind him and leans against it, satisfied that he has finally got the message. Looking up, she sees Rupert standing at the bottom of the stairs, a picture of misery, his forlorn face drawn and bleary with sleep, his bottom lip trembling.

"Rupert, what's the matter? Are you feeling sick?"

He shakes his head and stares at the floor.

Pamela frowns. "Rupert?"

He raises his head and looks to her. "When's Mummy coming home?"

Pamela is struck dumb. She goes to him, picks him up, and embraces him tightly. It's a very simple question. But she can't answer it.

Bundling Rupert into the car, she climbs into the driver's seat with purpose. Adjusting the rearview mirror, she catches her reflection and fixes herself with a look of resolve. She drives toward the city, with nothing to guide her but the overwhelming need to find Pamela Dickson. Rupert sits quietly in the back, sucking his thumb and clutching Kanga to himself. The asthma has passed, but the melancholy has taken a firm hold.

Reaching the city, Pamela searches for the place where the accident occurred. The shock must have blurred her memory of the details, but she knows that she'd been walking for some time in a westerly direction before she stepped off that fateful curb. Finally, the streets start looking familiar and she finds the intersection where Pamela had hit her. She can even see the young Christian hovering on the same corner, waiting with his clipboard to pounce on unsuspecting pedestrians.

She pulls over and studies the geography, working out exactly where she had been waiting and from which direction the car must have been coming. She looks at her watch. From what she can recall, it is almost the same time of day. Taking a deep breath, she pulls back into the traffic.

"Okay, Rupert, what I want you to do is close your eyes and think of Mummy. Okay? As hard as you can, I want you to picture Mummy in your head and wish with all your might for her to come back. Okay?"

Rupert nods and squeezes his eyes shut tightly without question. He is so completely trusting, she feels an aching rush of tenderness for this little boy who isn't really her own. She just hopes she won't disappoint him. They approach the corner.

"Okay. Start wishing until I tell you to stop."

As they go around the corner, Rupert wishes while Pamela chants to herself.

"Pamela, Pamela, Pamela . . ." She'd like to close her eyes, too, but she doesn't want to run over anyone who's not her. So she keeps her eyes peeled, but doesn't run over anything except an empty drink can. Pamela doesn't step out from anywhere, and the car makes it around the block without incident.

Rupert still has his eyes shut and is wishing very hard, so she goes around again. Still nothing. After the sixth time around she pulls over and leans her head on the steering wheel in despair. "Goddamn you, Pamela Dickson," she whispers.

Rupert opens his eyes expectantly. He looks at Pamela. "Do I still wish?"

She raises her head from the wheel and turns to him. "Time for a break. How about an ice cream?"

She unwraps the ice cream and hands it to Rupert. They sit on a bench in the street mall, Pamela sipping a take-away cappuccino, Rupert making a sloppy mess of his ice cream, and Kanga suffering the consequences. Pamela scoops up her froth with a plastic spoon, watching the passersby and wondering how many of them are haunted by regret.

Does that businessman over there with the shiny shoes and yellow tie regret that he hadn't had the courage to say hello to the woman on the bus this morning? Does that waitress at the cafe wish she'd listened to her parents and finished high school? Does that red-faced busker on the corner regret not taking up the violin as a child instead of the tuba?

Rupert drops his ice cream on the pavement with a splat. Pamela looks at the wasted sloppy mess and immediately regrets choosing an ice cream on a stick. She looks to Rupert, expecting tears. Instead, he is sitting bolt upright.

"Mummy!"

He clambers off the bench and runs away, while Pamela strains to see what he has seen, but she can see no one familiar among the crowds of shoppers. She throws her coffee into the trash bin next to her, grabs Kanga, and follows Rupert through the mall.

He runs as fast as his little legs can go. Pamela hangs back, knowing that Rupert is the key. He weaves his way through the pedestrians, around the corner, and into an arcade, where she loses sight of him.

"Rupert!"

She scans the crowds of shoppers for a little blond boy, kicking herself for being so irresponsible. She can't even remember what he is wearing.

"Rupert!"

She reaches the other end of the arcade, but there is no sign of him. Panic rising, she doubles back and checks the mall again. Then she sees him in the distance, standing alone, lost in the crowd, puffing and panting, tears streaming down his cheeks. She runs to him and picks him up, hugging him tightly.

"I saw her! I wished and wished!"

Pamela nods.

"Come on, sport. Let's go home."

In the half light of early dusk and under a cloud of despair, Pamela lies curled up on the bed. She can hear Stacy and Douglas fighting over the television remote control, and she wishes she had the energy to go out there and pull the plug out of the wall. But she hasn't. Instead, she blocks out the noise with a pillow and tries to block out her thoughts as well, but they keep on coming, like unforecast rain. She knows now that she is trapped in the life she thought she wanted. She's never going to find her other self, and she's never going to get home. Her mother was right when she told her as a child to be careful what she wished for. Well, Pamela sure has got it. She just wishes she had one more wish left.

Douglas barges into the bedroom without knocking. "What's for tea?"

Not moving, Pamela replies from under the pillow, her voice muffled, "I have no idea."

Douglas scowls. "What do you mean?"

"I mean, I'm not cooking."

"So, who is?"

She pulls her head from under the pillow. "Why don't you, for once?"

Douglas balks. "Me? But it's your job. I can't cook!"

She fixes him with an icy look. "Well, maybe you'd better learn."

When Robert gets home from work, he immediately senses something is wrong. His fears are confirmed when he enters the kitchen just in time to see Douglas with his head in the oven, trying to light a match.

"What the hell are you doing?"

Douglas pops his head out of the oven. "I can't find the clicker thing that you use to light the oven."

Robert confiscates the matches from him and closes the door of the oven, surveying the kitchen. Douglas has pulled out all the cans of food from the pantry and has poured a can of baked beans onto the top of a frozen pizza that he's forced into a casserole dish.

"What are you doing?"

Douglas grins proudly. "Making a pan pizza!"

Something is seriously wrong, and Robert is almost afraid to ask the next question. "Where's your mother?"

Douglas rolls his eyes. "I think she's sick."

Pamela must have dozed off, because when she awakens, it is dark and the house is silent. She switches on the bedside lamp and sits up. She can hear Brandy outside, howling to be fed.

In the deserted kitchen she pokes at Douglas's abandoned attempt at dinner and supposes that Robert has taken the children out for McDonald's. She scrapes half a tin of congealed dog food into the Bunnikins plate that still serves as Brandy's bowl. Then she dollops a couple of spoonfuls of Douglas's baked beans on top, as a treat.

Brandy wolfs down his dinner, particularly impressed by the baked beans, and wags his tail in appreciation. Pamela pats him on the head, then sits down on the back steps and looks past the treetops to the night sky. All at once she is filled with an acute sense of isolation, a strangling sensation in her throat, and a very strong urge to burst into tears. She reaches out and strokes Brandy, who is sniffing around the azaleas in an erratic after-dinner promenade.

Blowing her nose, she contemplates her feelings. She's never felt quite this way before. Or maybe once, when she was seven years old and she was supposed to stay at Julianne LeMercier's place overnight for a slumber party. It was a big adventure—her first time away from home. She didn't even make it past dinner before she rang up Mum and asked her to come and get her. Pamela remembers how she felt then, and she realizes what she is feeling now. Terrible, aching, homesickness.

As she turns off the laundry light, a pair of hands claps over her eyes and she is blinded. She screams with fright.

"Shh!"

She relaxes a little at the sound of Robert's voice, but she still hates not being able to see. She can hear the children giggling somewhere.

Keeping his hands over her eyes, Robert guides her to the door of her study. "Okay, you can look now."

He releases his hands, and Douglas and Stacy jump up from behind the desk. *"Surprise!"*

There on her desk is a brand-new computer with a big red-ribbon bow stuck on the top and a multitude of electronic "Happy Birthday"'s floating across the screen.

Robert waves at the computer. "It's not top of the line, but . . ."

". . . it should do for my purposes."

He stiffens. "It should be an improvement."

Pamela tries to smile, aware that she should be grateful. "Thank you. That's great. Really great."

She kisses him on the cheek and smiles at the kids.

Douglas is already rifling through the cardboard packing box. "Hey, look! We get free games with it! Cool!"

Pamela turns to Robert. "*We?*"

He shrugs guiltily. "I said maybe you might let them use it now and then." Before Pamela can respond, Robert claps his hands. "Okay, everyone in the car!"

Douglas won't sit still as they drive into the city. Pulling his seat belt to its limit, he leans between the front seats and bounces impatiently. "Where are we going?"

Robert turns to Douglas, practically bumping heads with him. "Sit back in your seat, Douglas."

"But where are we going? I'm hungry!"

"Somewhere special. It's a surprise. *Douglas!*" Douglas reluctantly sits back.

Stacy is equally curious. "Why is it such a secret?"

"Come on, Dad!"

Robert relents good-humoredly. "All right, all right, we're going back to your parents' old stamping ground." He puts a hand on Pamela's knee.

She peers out the window as they round a corner and sees a flashing neon sign. La Fontana.

"Charlie's?"

Douglas scowls. "I bet they don't do pan pizza."

Pamela can't believe her eyes. In this world, the run-down pizza joint she knows so well has been transformed by garish renovations.

Seeing Pamela's reaction, Robert nods in agreement. "The place isn't quite the same since Charlie won Lotto."

Pamela registers this slowly, trying to understand the twist.

Stacy helps her out. "Did he win millions? Who's Charlie?"

"Squillions. Poor old Charlie."

Douglas frowns. "Rich old Charlie, don't you mean?"

Pamela is equally confused.

Robert shakes his head. "Won a fortune, spent an absolute bomb on the restaurant, then went out and bought himself a brand-new Porsche—or was it a Ferrari?"

Pamela smiles. "A Ferrari. He loves Ferraris."

"Loved, you mean. That car was the end of him."

Pamela absorbs this remark with shock. Charlie is *dead?* She remembers him telling her how all his numbers nearly came up once. Well, apparently in this world they had. He'd got lucky and now he's gone. How cruel is that? Pamela fights back her tears as she tries to imagine La Fontana without the wiry old Chinese man.

Douglas pulls off his seat belt, annoyed. "Why couldn't we just go to Pizza Hut? What's so special about this place?"

"For your information, Douglas, you wouldn't be here if it wasn't for this place. This is where I proposed to your mother."

Douglas groans.

Stacy is intrigued. "Really? What did she say?"

Robert smiles and looks lovingly at Pamela. She tries to reciprocate.

Just Me, Pamela 15

Pamela peers over the top of her menu, unnerved by the new decor, for which no expense, if not taste, has been spared. Marbled columns, wisteria-covered archways, and a trompe l'oeil view of the Colosseum set the tone. But the pièce de résistance is the working model of the Fontana di Trevi, true to life, with the exception of the Harpic blue of the trickling water and the constant rasping of the pump that is barely disguised by the music of the sleepy mandolin player in the corner. This might have been Charlie's dream restaurant, but Pamela felt herself longing for faded laminated tables and plastic tablecloths with cigarette burns.

A jovial restaurant photographer does the rounds, encouraging young lovers to pose by the fountain, or families to stand in front of the Colosseum for a "holiday snap."

Robert puts his menu down and looks around cheerily. "This is great, isn't it?"

Pamela nods weakly.

Douglas glares suspiciously at the menu. "They're not pan pizzas."

Robert smiles. "Brings back memories. God, do you remember the last time we came here? Seems like another life."

"Yes, it does."

"Remember our table?"

She nods. They look across to the corner by the window, where a young couple holds hands across the table. That is where Robert proposed to Pamela all those years ago, the exact point where Pamela's life hit a fork in the road. She remembers making the tortured decision in the ladies' toilets, having left Robert sitting at the table for an indecent amount of time with only a jewel box and a glass of cheap claret for company. She came back from the bathroom and told him no over the tartuffo. She has never forgotten the wounded look that came into his eyes, and the way the tartuffo melted into a pool of chocolate, leaving the glacé cherry awash.

Robert turns back to the family and smiles, having dipped into more cheerful recollections. "I was thinking, what do you say we take a decent break at Christmas and rent the cottage down at the beach."

Douglas bounces in his seat. "Yes!"

"We haven't done that in years. Could be just what we need. Some time together . . . away from everything."

Stacy considers the idea skeptically. "Really? Would I be able to bring someone?"

Douglas boggles his eyes suggestively. "Oohh! What's his name?"

Stacy thumps him. Robert turns meaningfully to Pamela. "We could call it . . . a second honeymoon."

Pamela tenses. "A what?"

He hesitates, then reaches into his jacket pocket and pulls out a small velvet box, pushing it toward Pamela, almost shyly. Rupert starts jiggling in his seat and Stacy shrinks in hers.

"Oh, my God. How embarrassing."

Robert laughs. "Would you believe it? I almost feel as nervous as the first time."

Pamela stares at the box.

Robert nudges her. "Go on, open it."

Douglas leans on the table. "Open it! Open it, dumb——" He stops in his tracks. "Mum."

Pamela feels all eyes on her as she slowly opens the box, to find a gold wedding band set with diamonds. She stares at it, aghast.

Robert tries to gauge her reaction. "I know you're going to think this is a bit corny . . . but I was wondering . . . if you'd . . . if we . . ."

Stacy rolls her eyes. "Dad, you've got to get on your knees!"

Much to Pamela's horror, Robert does as he is told. Down on one knee, he takes her hand. "Hell, how about taking out an option on another thirteen years?"

Douglas groans. "Yuk! Will we have to go to a church and get dressed up?"

Stacy digs Douglas sharply in the ribs.

"Ow!"

Robert looks to Pamela, waiting anxiously for a response. He squeezes her hand, as if willing her to answer, but Pamela is speechless. This is all she used to dream of. A second chance to marry Robert Dickson, a chance to undo her past mistake and

203

say yes. She looks from Robert to Stacy to Douglas, all waiting for her to say yes. Then she looks at Rupert, a picture of disapproval. For him, it is clear that Daddy is dishing out diamond rings to the wrong woman. He looks at Pamela as if she has betrayed him.

Pamela's hesitation worries Robert, and his confidence dissipates as the seconds tick by. He gets up off his knees, takes the ring out of the box, holds it out to her, and smiles nervously. "Well? . . ."

She bites her lip. At that moment the roving photographer spots a romantic photo opportunity. "Photo, folks? Looks like you've got something to celebrate."

Pamela welcomes the rotund Englishman with uncharacteristic enthusiasm. "Great idea! What about a family portrait?"

Robert smiles weakly, knowing that things aren't going according to plan. He comforts himself with the thought that she took her time to answer the first time he proposed. He slips the ring back into the velvet box and nods to the photographer. "Why not?"

The photographer beams. "Great! Now, works best if we keep the happy couple together, then arrange the littlies around them."

Douglas jumps into position next to Pamela, wrapping his arms tightly around her neck, almost strangling her with affection until she can hardly breathe. Stacy hops up and stands behind them while the photographer gestures at Rupert.

"Why don't we have the little one on Daddy's knee?"

Robert waves Rupert over. "Come on, Rupert."

Rupert shakes his head vehemently. "I need to go to the toilet."

Stacy and Douglas groan impatiently, but Pamela rises eagerly from her seat, breaking free of Douglas's deadly grip. She grabs Rupert's hand, smiling apologetically. "Back in a minute."

Robert watches her as she hurries away, Rupert in tow. The ring remains in the open jewel box. He picks up his glass of wine and drains it.

Charlie's windfall stretched to marble vanities, brass fittings, and imported Italian tiles. Standing in the corners of the bathroom are gilded pedestals, topped with shiny ceramic urns bursting with top-quality imitation hydrangeas. It's a far cry from the grubby ladies' loo at Charlie's pizzeria, where the cisterns run chronically and the toilet paper doubles as hand towels. But, at least there, Charlie is alive to complain to.

Pamela opens the door into a pristine fruits-of-the-forest perfumed cubicle, then follows Rupert in. He turns around indignantly, pushes her out of the cubicle, shuts the door with a bang, and locks it behind him.

She goes to the basins, closes her eyes, and takes a deep breath. What the hell is she going to do? How's she going to go back out there and face Robert? She knows in her heart that she can't wear that ring. She can't say yes and she can't marry him again, just as she couldn't marry him in the first place. But where does that leave Robert and the kids? Is she really going to end up as a divorced mother of three in a world where she doesn't belong?

She turns on the Cold tap hard, leans over, and soaks her face, just as she did thirteen and a half years earlier, when Robert first asked for her hand in marriage. Now, as the icy water splashes her face, she suddenly remembers with perfect clarity all the reasons she had for turning him down, plus all the reasons for saying yes. Pamela realizes for the first time in her life that she hadn't made the wrong choice at all. Nor had she made the right choice. She had simply made *a* choice. And somewhere along the way, she had lost the courage to live by it. Today she must make another choice, but this time, whatever she decides, she knows that she must stick to it.

She turns off the water and calmly contemplates her dripping reflection in the mirror. Then she contemplates her other reflection. She freezes. There, in the mirror, directly behind her, stands another her.

Pamela is careful not to blink, let alone move, for fear that the reflection will evaporate. She stares at the reflection, confused. She knows it must be Pamela Dickson, but it looks more like Pamela Drury. Her hair is cut short, just like Pamela's, and she is wearing Pamela's leather jacket.

Pamela can stay still no longer. She must know if she is looking at the real thing or at a phantom of her imagination. She wheels around and, sure enough, Pamela Dickson is standing there, in the flesh, feet planted firmly on Charlie's imported Italian tiles. Pamela goes weak at the knees and her eyes fill with tears of relief. Pamela Dickson smiles, which results in Pamela having the sudden urge to punch her in the face.

"Where the hell have you been?"

Pamela Dickson's smile fades.

Rupert calls from inside the cubicle. "What did you say?"

Both Pamelas glance toward the cubicle. "Nothing, Rupert."

Pamela turns back to Pamela Dickson, lowering her voice to a whisper. *"Well? What happened?"*

Pamela Dickson gestures vaguely. "I don't know."

"You don't *know?*"

Pamela kicks herself for forgetting to whisper.

Rupert calls out again. "What?"

"Nothing, Rupert. I'm just . . . talking to myself."

She looks back to Pamela Dickson, who seems to be in a state of confusion equal to her own. "*Well?*"

Pamela Dickson shakes her head helplessly, staring at the floor. "I don't know what happened. You were there . . . the kids came home from school . . . then suddenly— I guess I must've . . . I had to . . . find out."

Pamela doesn't comprehend. "Find out what?"

Pamela Dickson takes a breath. "What would've happened if I'd said no to Robert. What if I hadn't had children? What would it feel like to have my own money, my own time, my own *bed?*" She meets Pamela's gaze. "Did you think I never wondered what it would feel like to be able to sit down and read a whole book, or a whole chapter, or even a whole *page* without being interrupted? To remember who I am—not Darling or Mummy or Dummy or Mum. Just *me,* Pamela. Like you."

Pamela is stunned.

Pamela Dickson shakes her head ashamedly. "This is all my fault. I'm sorry. I guess I was so full of questions and doubts and regrets that I somehow sucked you out of your life and into mine."

Pamela considers this. "No. It wasn't just you. I think I might have sucked, too."

They are reminded that they are not alone when Rupert pulls vigorously at the toilet-paper dispenser. Pamela Dickson looks at Pamela in surprise, impressed by this development in his personal-hygiene skills.

207

Pamela shrugs self-deprecatingly. "I think he probably decided he couldn't do a worse job than me."

Pamela Dickson smiles, peeling off the leather jacket and holding it out to Pamela. They start to exchange clothes hastily, but Pamela is not satisfied.

"What happened—with me and Robert?"

Pamela Dickson regards her frankly, as if it should be obvious. "Just the usual. One minute it was candlelit dinners for two and sushi on the beach, and the next we're wading in poopy diapers and dealing with sore nipples, baby vomit, no sleep, short tempers and measles and asthma, and working and organizing and worrying and totally surrendering to these creatures that for some obscure reason you love more than anything else in the world. Stick a relationship through that. It doesn't come out the same as it went in."

She finishes buttoning her shirt as Pamela pulls on the leather jacket.

"I know Robert and I lost the plot along the way. We need to work through some . . . problems. But I still love him, if that's what you want to know."

Pamela nods solemnly. "Good, because I don't think you'll be seeing much more of Geoffrey Ballodero."

Pamela Dickson grimaces, embarrassed in front of herself. "I really don't know how that happened."

Pamela smiles, uncharacteristically understanding. "Don't worry. You should see some of the jerks I've wound up in bed with!"

The toilet flushes and Pamela quickly adjusts Pamela Dickson's hair and throws her some last-minute advice. "Now, don't you let Douglas get away with that 'dummy' stuff. You might want to buy Stacy a jar of Vaseline, and . . . , uh . . . I think you'd better start looking for another job."

Pamela Dickson catches Pamela's hand in her own. She looks into Pamela's eyes. "Thank you."

The Engaged sign on the toilet switches to Vacant, and Rupert emerges, adjusting his trousers. He goes to a basin, stands on tiptoes, and holds his little hands under the tap. Pamela Dickson turns on the tap for him, her eyes shining with emotion.

Rupert washes his hands carefully. He shakes them dry, then looks up to Pamela Dickson for the first time. His face lights up with joy. "Mummy!"

A sob of emotion escapes her as she bends down and scoops the little boy into her arms, kissing him fervently. Rupert hugs his mother as if he'll never let go. She swings him onto her hip and carries him from the bathroom. He glances behind him as the door swings closed.

Pamela steps out from the shadows of the last cubicle.

Wiggling out of his mother's arms, Rupert runs at breakneck speed back to the table where Robert sits, anxiously playing with his glass of wine. "Daddy! Daddy! Mummy's back! She's back!"

He tugs Robert's sleeve excitedly. Robert looks at the little boy inquiringly. Pamela Dickson arrives at the table and takes her seat, smiling fondly at the children and running her hand tenderly through Stacy's hair.

Stacy grimaces. "Mum! Get off!"

She turns to Robert, who is watching her intently. Then she notices the open jewel box in front of her. Her eyes widen at the sight of the diamond wedding band.

209

Robert takes the ring from the box, then takes her hand. "May I?"

She looks into Robert's eyes, guessing the significance of the moment, and her eyes fill with tears. She hesitates, then nods sincerely. "Yes."

Robert slides the ring onto her finger and kisses her on the lips. Then he takes a gulp of wine to calm his nerves. She had given him a scare. Just like the first time.

The night air is cool and crisp. Pamela shivers and pulls her jacket tightly around her as she watches the restaurant from across the street. Inside, Robert beckons to the photographer.

As the photographer is arranging the family for their portrait, Rupert clambers down from his mother's knee and comes to the window. Seeing Pamela outside, he presses his hand against the glass. Her eyes prick with tears and she is surprised by the strength of her feelings for the child who had known all along that she was an imposter. She raises her hand in farewell.

"Rupert!"

Robert calls him back to the table and lifts him into position for the photo. The photographer makes some last-minute adjustments while Robert leans close to his wife, puts his arm around her, and kisses her. She smiles and kisses him back.

Pamela watches Pamela Dickson nestle happily into Robert Dickson's arms and whispers, "Thank *you*."

The photographer is ready. The family poses and Douglas pulls a face. The camera flashes at the exact moment that the "William Tell Overture" starts playing. Pamela jumps at the piercing music. Reaching into her pockets, she pulls out her mobile phone. She regards it quizzically, like an object from the distant past.

"Hello? . . . Mum! . . . What? . . . No, I'm just . . . out . . . Dinner? . . . When? Who might call me? . . . No, I'm sure he's very nice . . . Look . . . Mum . . . can I call you later? I promise. 'Bye."

She flips the phone shut, looks back to the restaurant, and is startled to see that it has been transformed back into Charlie's run-down pizza joint. And she can make out Charlie inside, glued to the Lotto draw on the decrepit television above the fridge. It is obvious by the look on his face that he hasn't won. He tears up his card and sucks mournfully on his cigarette. Pamela smiles. She backs away from the pizzeria, turns, and heads home.

It's not until she rounds the corner of her street and sees her apartment block just as she left it that she starts to breathe freely. No scaffolding, no building site, and no flashy billboard, just a dilapidated 1940s redbrick block of flats in desperate need of some loving attention. She pushes through the security doors and takes the steps to the top floor, two at a time.

Sliding her key into the lock, she opens the door and switches on the hallway light. Surveying the living room, she is relieved to see the familiar mess of incomplete renovations, tins of paint, brushes, sandpaper, heat gun, drop sheets, used coffee cups, take-away containers, discarded newspapers. She walks up to the half-stripped wardrobe and gazes into the mirror, half expecting to see the Dicksons' bedroom in the reflection. But all she can see is a very weary and shell-shocked Pamela Drury staring her in the face.

Peeling off her jacket and kicking off her shoes on the way to the bedroom, she passes the answering machine and automatically presses play.

"Hi, it's Terri. I'm going to have to give tomorrow's walk a miss. Otto's teething and not very happy about it. Sorry. Talk soon."

Beep.

"Pam, Max. Look, I need to discuss this article, 'What Do Girls Want?.' To be blunt, it reads like a piece of pap from a woman's glossy. Ring me ASAP."

Beep.

"Pam, it's your mother. I'll try your mobile."

Beep.

The messages flow over her, unheard. Entering the bedroom, she closes the door soundly behind her and falls headlong onto her double bed.

Me Myself I 16

The morning sunshine streams through the bedroom window and across Pamela's comatose body in dust-speckled shafts of light. She rolls over, the night's sleep imprinted onto her creased face. Groggily, she half opens her eyes as she awakens from a very deep sleep. Listening for the sound of Robert's snoring, she concludes that he must already be up. But after a few moments she wonders why she can hear traffic noise and car horns instead of morning birdsong. She rubs her eyes open and wearily surveys her surroundings, gradually recognizing her own bed, her own bedroom, and her own dirty clothes strewn across the floor. Traffic noise filters through the window, and on the bedside table sits a white toy kangaroo that is watching over her. She reaches for the toy and slowly runs her hands over its pristine fur. Its two original glass eyes gaze up blankly at her. Pamela shakes her head sadly. That has to be the most vivid and profound dream she has ever had in her whole life. She must remember to write it down before she forgets it.

Leaping out of bed, she wraps herself in her dear old terry-cloth bathrobe and inserts her favorite Aretha Franklin into the CD player. Bursting with inexplicable energy, she wiggles and grooves her way into the kitchen, puts some coffee on, and scrounges in the kitchen drawers for all the garbage bags she can find.

"R-E-S-P-E-C-T, find out what it means to me . . ."

She doesn't know quite why she feels so motivated today, but she cleans and tidies the flat with great gusto, filling eight giant green garbage bags with all the rubbish that she has let accumulate since she moved in. She is horrified by the number of take-away pizzas she must have eaten lately. She is also surprised to find several ashtrays full of cigarette butts that she has no memory of smoking. She dumps the butts out, then tosses the ashtrays out, as well. Moving on, she empties a hidden box full of singles magazines, personal ads, and photographs, and she takes great pleasure in tearing them up and bagging them. Oddly, she knows with complete and utter certainty that her days of moping around and worrying about being single are well and truly over. She has no idea what the future holds for her, but she knows it won't be filled with wishing for what isn't.

She picks up her entire collection of saucepans off the floor and dumps their contents—rusty rainwater—down the drain before returning them to the kitchen. Then she flips open the Yellow Pages and looks up Dynamite Roofs and Plumbing, making an appointment for the following day.

Next, she goes through her dressing-table drawers and empties all her out-of-date medication into a garbage bag. Caught up in the pure blood-pumping exhilaration of clearing clutter, she makes the bold decision to chuck anything she hasn't used within the last year: makeup, airline toiletries, nail polish, junk jewelery, sample moisturizers, expired condoms. She stubbornly resists the urge to sneak things back into the drawers "just in case."

Dragging a bulging garbage bag from her bedroom, she dumps it by the door and searches for a fresh one as she sings along to Aretha and Annie Lennox. "Sisters Are Doing It for Themselves."

She pulls out a bag and shakes it open, heading for the bathroom, which is next on the agenda. Pamela eyes the hair dryer lying on the floor, remembering with shame the last time she held it in her hands. She shudders as she plugs it into the wall, then stands well back and flicks the switch with a wooden ruler. Nothing results but a pop and a *phut* and the nasty smell of a burned element. Pulling the cord out of the wall and dropping the dryer into the garbage bag, she reminds herself to dig out the spare travel dryer she bought last time she went overseas.

Opening the bathroom cabinet, she is faced with a glass jar full of toothbrushes in varying conditions. After picking out the newest one, a blue brush with bristles more or less intact, she boldly tosses the others into the rubbish. She follows these with three rolled-up tubes of toothpaste and an airline mini-toothpaste that she hates the taste of but had been keeping in case of an emergency. She proceeds to empty almost the entire contents of the cabinet, allowing herself to salvage only absolute essentials.

With a flourish, she removes the self-affirmations from the bathroom mirror and drops them ceremoniously into the rubbish.

"I *do* love and approve of myself. I *do* deserve the best and accept the best, and I *am* in the rhythm and flow of ever-changing life. So, there!"

Ten green-plastic garbage bags stuffed full of a year's worth of rubbish sit exiled on the landing outside Pamela's apartment. Inside, she is sweeping newly vacated floor space that hasn't seen the light of day since she moved in. She's been cleaning and tidying like a maniac all day, possessed by a notion that she's had since awakening from her dream—the embarrassingly clichéd, but nevertheless marvelous belief that today actually *is* the first day of the rest of her life.

Bone-tired and completely caked in dust and grime, she shrugs off her bathrobe and steps into the shower. The hot water sluices away the dirt and exhaustion, and before she knows it she's humming a ditty from *South Pacific*. "I'm gonna wash that man right outta my hair . . . and send him on his way. . . ."

The shampoo lid slips from her hands, and she bends to pick it up. The soap starts washing into her eyes, so she shuts them tightly while she gropes for the lid, which is traveling toward the plug hole. Then she comes across something in the drain that she doesn't recognize by feel. Must be the washer, fallen off the tap again. She sighs. Standing up, she reaches for a towel and wipes her eyes. She squints at the object in her hand. It's not a washer. It's a ring. A gold wedding ring. She stares at it, stunned. She slips it onto her wedding finger. It fits.

Startled by the telephone, she turns off the shower and stumbles into the living room, naked and dripping wet.

"Hello?"

"Finally got the courage to pick up the phone, hey?"

She recognizes the gruff Irish accent.

"This bloody article on girls! Honestly, Pam!"

She grimaces. "Oh, that. Sorry, Max. I haven't—"

"I should bloody well think so. What were you playing at?"

"What do you mean?"

"It's crap—that's what I mean. You know we can't print this kind of rubbish! You'd be better off trying to sell it to a women's glossy."

Pamela's blood chills. She doesn't even remember finishing the article, let alone delivering it to Max, and she knows that what she had written certainly wasn't crap. But she also knows someone who is capable of writing the kind of copy Max is referring to.

She plays with the ring on her finger, trying to deny the growing realization that something has been going on while she was dreaming. She knows she hasn't eaten that many take-away pizzas lately, and she certainly hasn't smoked that many cigarettes. She's been trying to block out the growing suspicion that someone else has been in her flat, but now she can't ignore it.

"I'm really sorry, Max. I haven't been . . . feeling well. You'll have another version by next week."

"Forget it, Pam. Who cares what girls want, anyway? Why don't you take a week or two off? Sounds like you need it. Don't want you burning out and ending up in a loony bin, do we?"

"No . . . we don't."

So, it wasn't a dream. She sits at the kitchen table with a glass of red wine, trying to let the reality soak in. It's no surprise really. It didn't seem like a dream when she was in it, and it isn't fading like a dream now. She's not frightened by the idea. If anything, she is filled with a sense of elation. She always felt cheated by those stories, like *The Wizard of Oz* or *Alice in Wonderland,* in which the whole adventure turned out to be a dream.

No, this time she really had followed the white rabbit—or,

217

in this case, kangaroo—into the other world. The world of
Pamela Dickson. And Robert, Stacy, Douglas, and Rupert.

She wonders what they are all doing at this moment. And
she wonders what will become of them, suspecting that she'll
never find out how that side of the story ends. Nor should she.
She was privileged to glimpse their world, however briefly, and
she was privileged to make a new acquaintance. Herself. Maybe
one day she'll write it all down. Who knows, maybe one day
someone, somewhere, will read her story and actually believe
it. But she doubts it.

She pours out the last of the wine and raises her glass. "To
Narnia."

After covering the floors with old bedsheets and newspapers, she attacks the renovations with newfound enthusiasm.
Now there is nothing stopping her. The days pass quickly as
she rips the old wallpaper off the walls to the sounds of talkback radio and daytime television, scrapes the stubborn bits,
then washes down the walls until her arms drop off. She sands
and fills and paints and sands and fills and paints, leaving the
flat only for food and hardware supplies. In the living room she
opts for fresh, clean white walls and woodwork, but for the
kitchen she chooses warm yellows and blues. She steps back to
appraise the colors and realizes she has reproduced exactly the
color scheme of the Dickson kitchen. She smiles. Only the finger paintings are missing.

Finally, she cleans up the brushes and rollers, picks up the
drop sheets, and moves the furniture back into place. She dusts
off all her pictures, hangs them, and brings her potted plants in
off the balcony. Sorting through the boxes of books that have

been languishing for want of shelves, she relegates any that come under the self-help category to the charity box. Then she packs the rest away again, promising that shelves are imminent. The boxes glare at her. She justifies that she has to keep a project up her sleeve for a rainy day. . . .

But there is one project she can't leave. The wardrobe. It takes her a whole weekend to strip the five layers of paint her younger selves had inflicted upon it. She blasts and sands and oils and polishes, until it looks almost as good as Pamela Dickson's. Last, she hangs the mirrored door and cleans the glass. Closing the doors, she stands back and admires it. She hardly recognizes herself in the mirror. She seems different. She seems . . . grown up.

In her local news stand, she walks right past the glossies, the bridal magazines, women's health and pregnancy, and stops at the cooking section. Picking up the latest issue of *Gourmet Traveller,* she flips through the mouth-watering recipes, which, without exception, require exotic ingredients and culinary finesse. She decides to buy *Gourmet Traveller* for her coffee table, and a copy of *Let's Start Cooking* for herself.

Overloaded with bags of groceries, she stops by the flower shop, just managing to squeeze a bunch of bright orange calendula under her arm.

Outside La Fontana, Charlie wipes down the tables, cigarette hanging from his lips. "Hey, Pamela! Coming in for some cannelloni tonight? Fresh today!"

Pamela turns and grins at Charlie. "No, thanks, Charlie. Not tonight. I'm cooking."

Charlie raises his eyebrows in surprise.

Backing through the entrance doors of her apartment

block, she juggles her shopping as she checks her letter box. Clamping the mail between her teeth, she flips the box shut with an elbow, turns to go up the stairs, and screams in fright, the mail slipping from her mouth. There, on the landing, sits Ben Monroe. Pamela is speechless.

Ben stands up sheepishly. "Hi."

"Ben . . ."

She loses her grip on her shopping and a bag of fruit and vegetables hits the floor, sending oranges, onions, bell peppers, and potatoes flying in all directions. She stares at the scattered groceries, dazed.

Ben hurries to help her pick them up. "Look, I know technically I shouldn't be here. . . ."

She shakes her head. "Are you for real?"

"I know, I know. Maybe I'm doing the wrong thing."

She watches as he repacks her shopping.

"I admit it might've been a mistake bringing the kids on our first date—"

Pamela starts. "Date?"

"And Molly throwing up on you like that. I can see that it might've put you off."

"*Kids?*" Pamela shakes her head. This conversation is not making sense.

She realizes with a sinking feeling that this isn't the Ben she thought it was. This isn't the gorgeous, available journalist Ben who's traveled across worlds to get to her. No, this is the gorgeous married Student Crisis Counselor Ben to whom she foolishly sent an invitation one dark and rainy night. He must have called her while Pamela Dickson was there. And she doesn't mind betting that Pamela Dickson made hay while the sun shone . . . just as she herself had done with Ben in the other world. Unfortunately, each scenario is as impossible as the other, and Pamela Dickson must have realized the same thing. She picks up her bags, leaving a stray orange on the floor. Ben picks it up and holds it out to her, but she backs away.

"Look, Ben, I don't expect you to understand, but whatever I've done or said lately . . . I . . . wasn't . . . myself."

He nods, without understanding. "Tell me you're not interested, and I'll leave you alone."

Stopping at the stairs, she stares at him aghast. "What about Sophie?"

Ben frowns. "Sophie?"

"The love of your life!"

"The *what?*"

"You know—marriage, kids, matching pajamas!"

He looks blankly at her. "What are you—"

"Your wife! She's alive, right?"

He shakes his head. "*Ex*-wife, you mean. And she's really very nice, but if you want me to have her killed, I guess I can look into it."

Pamela takes this in.

Ben smiles. "I know it's not simple. And I know you weren't looking for an instant family. The fact is, I do have the kids half the time. But Molly hardly ever vomits—I swear."

Pamela thinks of the journalist who has been wasting his life mourning the loss of a happy-ever-after that turns out to be a never-was.

Disheartened by her lack of response, Ben stares at the orange in his hand as he says, "Look, I haven't done this for a while. I just wanted to ask you if you'd give it another go. Do something, sometime. Go dancing, shoot some pool. I could cook you dinner."

"Dinner?"

He looks earnestly at her. "Obligation-free."

She turns away, trying to absorb this development.

Ben sighs and backs down the stairs. "I guess not."

He heads toward the door, but Pamela calls after him. "Can they wipe their own bottoms?"

He is caught off guard. "One can. The other one can be a bit hit-and-miss."

"Not that it bothers me."

He smiles. "Don't worry, that's my job."

"I mean, I can do it when I have to."

He holds up his hands. "No bottoms!"

Pamela nods.

Ben is bemused. "So . . . is that a maybe?"

She considers a moment, then nods solemnly. "That's a maybe!"

He lingers. "And could we be talking this weekend?"

Pamela shrugs. For once in her life she feels in no hurry. "Could be."

He smiles, tossing the orange up into the air and catching it with a flourish. "See you then."

"See you."

He opens the door.

Pamela frowns. "Hey!"

He turns.

She looks sternly at him. "That's my orange."

Ben looks at the orange and goes to toss it to her but sees that her arms are full. He climbs the first flight of stairs and drops it into her bag of shopping. On impulse she leans over the railing and kisses him ardently before breaking the clinch and continuing up the stairs. Stunned, Ben watches after her.

Closing the door to her flat, she drops her shopping on the hall table. A smile steals across her face. Running to the window, she peers through the blinds and watches Ben walk away down the street. He turns and glances up at her window, but Pamela ducks out of sight.

She goes to open the window, but it won't budge. Layers of paint have sealed it closed.

"Shit!"

Pulling out her toolbox, she attacks the window with a hammer and chisel. Finally, it budges a little. She puts all her might into it and suddenly the window opens wide with an ear-splitting screech.

Pamela leans out the window and looks up over the rooftops to a perfectly blue sky. A moment's peace. A future full of possibilities. She smiles.